Pillow Talk Will Get You Killed

By: Caryn Lee

PILLOW TALK WILL GET YOU KILLED

- Written by -

CARYN LEE

Facebook: https://www.facebook.com/caryndeniselee?fref=ts

Cover design/Graphics: Micah Designer Shipp

ACKNOWLEDGEMENTS

Giving praises to God first and foremost, without him I will still be afraid to write. This is now my 8th novel and my first street story. I enjoyed writing this novel and stepping away from the romance and drama literature. Don't get me wrong it's still some romance and drama mixed in the storyline. Laughing I couldn't leave that out. I would love to thank all of the READERS! You have been the biggest supporters throughout my writing career. Thank you for always rocking with and reading my work. To the readers that follow me on Facebook, thank you for the extra push!!!! I'm not dropping any names in this Acknowledgements, please don't be mad. I just want to thank everyone who has supported me from my family, friends, and the readers!!! Please enjoy my latest novel PILLOW TALK WILL GET YOU KILLED! Chicago please put the guns down!!!!!

Prologue

That's that nigga right there." Ty said nodding his head in the direction of their next come up.

"Yeah I see all those flashy niggas. They definitely getting money. Yo, where the hell is Sunshine at? She still down with the mother fucking plan or what?" Bari asked he was amped up and high off the pill.

"Yeah, she's still down. I hollered at the hoe earlier."

Ty and Bari were sitting back in the cut in an all-black Chevy Caprice watching Duke and his people pull up to the club. Duke was their next target on the list. They watched him as he jumped out of his 2015 Bentley and walked inside the club with his entourage following behind him. Moments later a red Infiniti G35 pulled up and stopped in front of the club entrance. Out stepped Sunshine as she passed the valet attendant her keys and cash.

"There goes Sunshine ass right there," said Ty smiling while he rubbed his palms together.

"Got damn Sunshine thick ass hell. She looking good tonight, bitch starting to make my dick hard." Bari said grabbing his crouch.

Sunshine was a thick red bone that worked with us from the Southside. All the niggas couldn't resist her. She stood at 5'5", weighing 139lbs, and her measurements are 38-24-42. They called her Sunshine because she had a yellow pussy that shined bright like the sun. We heard that Duke had a thing for light skin bitches, so we used the bitch to catch Duke's eye and the shit worked. They have been dating for a month now and the nigga has already flown her out of the country, took her to meet his parents, and tonight his sweet ass was taking her to his crib. Tonight was the night that we planned on making our hit. After the party it was going down, I was thirsty for this hit. If the shit that Sunshine told us was true then we would have enough cash and drugs to split up and to start doing our own thing. We sat in the car and I went over the plan with Bari once again.

Sunshine switched her phat ass as she walked through the club making her way to VIP. Duke, his crew, and a few women were sitting at the table. "Excuse me," said Sunshine to a brown skin chick who was whispering into Duke's ear. She turned to look at Sunshine and rolled her eyes as she walked off. She knew that she wasn't any competition when it came to her.

"Hey, baby." Duke said grabbing Sunshine by her tiny waist and rubbing her ass.

"Hey, daddy. What I tell you about having basic bitches all in your face?" Sunshine said.

"Chill out with all that, you know that you're my baby. These other chicks don't have anything on you." Duke said making Sunshine head bigger than it was already.

One of Duke's friends came over to holler at him. Sunshine sat off to the side as she tried to ear hustle. With the music being so loud she couldn't hear what they were talking about. It was cracking in the club tonight and all the hoes were out. Sunshine peeped a few of the thirsty hoes who were whispering and pointing at Duke as if he was a celebrity. She waved at the two ladies with a smile on her face. They smirked, gave her the middle finger, and turned their heads. 'You hoes won't be coming up tonight', she thought to herself. Moments later ten bartenders made their way through the crowd carrying buckets filled with bottles that sparkled on the top. Everyone watched them as they placed the buckets onto our table.

"Can we get you anything else Duke?" asked one of the women.

"Once we finished these I'll be needing ten more," said Duke.

"Cool just let me know and I will be glad to assist you." The woman smiled as Duke slid her a one hundred dollar bill. She put the money inside her bra.

Sunshine poured herself a glass of alcohol. As Duke entertained his company she pulled her cell phone out to send Ty a text message.

Sunshine: I'm here now

Ty: Cool, let me know when you leave

Sunshine put her phone back into her clutch. Duke had now drawn his attention to her. "You look amazing tonight. I can't wait to get you home to fuck the shit out of you."

"I can't wait to bounce up and down on that dick daddy," Sunshine said.

She opened her legs just enough for her yellow pussy to peep at him. Duke licked his lips, "Damn it's like that?!" He took one of his fingers dipping it inside her tight pussy. Sunshine giggled and moaned, "Yes daddy it's like that."

Meanwhile, two hours later Ty and Bari sat in the car smoking on some Kush as they watched all the activity from afar. Bari was pumped up and was starting to become impatient. While Ty was calm and counted the money in his head.

"Damn nigga how much longer are they going to be in there?" Bari asked.

"Man nigga just chill we have all night." Ty said looking at him as if he was crazy and shook his head.

"I got to piss!" Bari jumped out of the car and walked behind the tree to piss. Ty phone vibrated, it was a text message from Sunshine.

Sunshine: We r leaving now

Ty: Cool

Bari sat back inside the car. Ty told him that Sunshine and the Duke lame ass was finally leaving. Duke and his people stepped outside and got in their luxury vehicles. Before leaving he made sure that Sunshine was inside her car. After that, Duke pulled off with Sunshine and his crew following behind them as they hopped onto the Dan Ryan. Sunshine called and told me what the plan was. We followed a distanced behind them, giving them some space trying not to tip them off. Shortly after the two cars that were following Duke exited. Now it was only Sunshine who was following him. They finally arrived at Duke's place in University Park. I hollered at Sunshine before she went in the house with her to go over everything. Bari and I sat in the car parked a block away as we waited for Sunshine to give us the say so to come inside.

Inside the house, Sunshine and Duke was getting cozy and shit. Duke was starting to feel soft for Sunshine. Sunshine didn't waste any time as she undressed and teased Duke with her juicy body. Duke laid in the bed with a hard dick ready to fuck the shit out of her. She straddled him and kissed on his ear lobe. Duke kissed her softly on the lips and gazed into her eyes.

"Baby you're amazing. I was going to wait to give you your gift tomorrow, but I guess that now would be a good time." Duke went inside his safe and grabbed a box.

Sunshine eyes grew with excitement when she noticed the ring that Duke presented to her. It was a nice four-carat diamond ring. She has received many gifts in the past from several men, but no one has ever given her a ring. Suddenly Sunshine didn't want to go ahead with setting up Duke. At that moment, she had a change of heart about getting up and unlocking the back door. This could be a major change in her life, no more tricking off and setting up niggas to rob them. Sunshine was ready to leave all that bullshit alone and start a new life with Duke. Thirty minutes had gone by, Ty and Bari was starting to question Sunshine's actions. When she didn't text them back giving them the word they both knew what they had to. Ty and Bari took it upon themselves to go ahead with the plan anyway. They put on their masks and broke into Duke's backdoor without signaling off his alarm. They crept up his stairs and allowed the sounds of love making to lead the way. Ty peeped into the slightly adjourned door and witness Sunshine riding Duke. She didn't even see what was coming, in the back of her mind, she thought that the two wouldn't go on with the plan if they didn't hear from her. In a matter of seconds, Ty and Bari busted into the door with their guns pointed at them.

"Don't your bitch ass even think about making that move!" Bari said as Duke tried to reach for his gun.

Sunshine starting screaming and crying acting as if she didn't know what was happening. Ty was busy inside of Duke's closet cleaning out his safe stuffing as much money as he could into his duffle bag. He took some of his jewelry and two guns.

Pop! Pop! Pop! Pop! Noooo please don't shoot me!"
Sunshine screamed.

Ty stopped and ran out of the closet. Duke and Sunshine
were leaned over slumped in bed and covered in blood.

"What the fuck did you?" Ty asked Bari.

"Man he tried reaching for his gun and Sunshine was trying
to help him," Bari said.

"Come on man we have to get out of here now!" Ty said.

They both ran out of the house with the money, drugs,
jewelry and guns that they confiscated. Shooting Sunshine
was not a part of the plan. Ty didn't know what exactly had
gone down because he was busy inside of the closet. They
made it back to the car and drove off in silence. Bari turned
on the radio, but Ty angrily turned off the music.

"What the fuck is wrong with you man?!" Bari said.

"Sunshine, that's what's wrong!" Ty said.

"Man I know that you're not tripping over that hoe. She
tried to help Duke bitch ass and got what she deserved."
Bari said.

From what I heard inside the closet Sunshine was
screaming for Bari not to shoot her. I can't believe that

Sunshine had turned on us in the middle of our hit. She has never let us down in the past when it came down to business. Apart of me felt bad for her, but the moment when she switched up on us she had to go. Bari was amped up and got a kick out of killing the both of them. He turned on the music and rolled up a blunt as I sped down the highway. Damn! Another one bites the dust, but I wasn't expecting Sunshine to join him. She was only supposed to trick the nigga into liking her and not fall in love with him. The last time that I got up with Sunshine I could tell by the look in her eyes when she spoke about him that she was feeling Duke. I strictly told her ass to suck and fuck as much information out of his ass. It didn't take long for Duke to fall under Sunshine's spell and for him to start pillow talking. Once we heard about how much money that he kept in his safe it was time for us to make a move. In the beginning Sunshine was ready to stick and move around. I wonder what got in her head from the moment that she left the club till the moment when she made it to his house. In this game you can't switch sides, the consequences could cost you your life.

Chapter 1

Tichina

It was a hot summer day in the Chi. I was outside hanging with my two best friends Emani and Kamara. We were sitting on Emani's front porch watching the children play outside. Where we live in Chicago you have to keep an eye out on your children. At any minute, it could get crazy out here and bullets could get to flying. Living here you learn how to survive, but your life isn't promised. On a weekly basis, we are attending more funerals than graduations. Small children are going to their friend birthday party one day and then the next day their funerals. It's a blessing to live to see another day. By the way, my name is Tichina Jefferson. I'm 26 years old, soft on the outside but hard on the inside. I'm light skinned, short and I weigh 143lbs. Growing up being the only child could be boring at times, but lucky for me I had my two best friends. I met Kamara and Emani in the first grade. We were from the Westside of Chicago, but our parents bused us to school on the Northside so that we could have a better education. The moment that we sat down in class and seen that we were the only three black girls we bonded immediately. I'm happy to say that after all these years that we are still connected together. While growing up I was blessed to have both parents in my life. My mother and father have been together since they were twenty years old. Both of my parents were strict and I was never able to do anything. It was like being in jail. I never understood why my parents were so hard on me until one day when a painful event happened. At the young age of 15 I was so in love with my boyfriend Marcus. I trusted him with my heart and was down for him. We were drinking and I didn't know that Marcus had slipped something into my drink. The last thing that I remember was that I was laughing and sitting on the couch. Next thing you know I woke up naked and fighting Marcus and his two friends off of me. I was too weak to fight them off of me. Every time when I would swing or punch them, it felt as if I was moving in slow motion. Before they all raped me I begged them to put on a condom. I know that it may sound strange, but I didn't want to catch anything. After convincing them that wearing a condom will be a smart thing to do the three of them raped me one by one, entering every hole in my body. Marcus left me in his basement locked up for two days only feeding me Ramen noodles and raping me repeatedly. It wasn't a phone, window, or no way that I could get out. I would scream and holler, but no one would hear me. The only thing that saved me was a screwdriver. The next time when Marcus tried to rape me I pulled out the screwdriver that I was hiding under the pillow and stabbed him with it. I ran away upstairs and got away. To make the situation crazy his parents were there and was in shock when they saw me naked and bruised. After that whole ordeal, all three of them were charged and arrested. They were sent off to the Juvenile Detention Center until they turned twenty-one years old. I've carried so much pain inside of me. Being raped at such a young age caused me to have trust issues when it came to men. Every time when I meet someone new I keep it real with them by telling them upfront that I was solvent. In the beginning, they are cool with it, but after a while they always try to persuade me into having sex with them. Needless to say, it never works out and I just gave up on dating. I want something more than sex and I'm willing to keep my closed until the right man comes into my life.

Now that I have introduced myself, let me get back to me and my two best friends sitting on the porch. It was a hot Saturday afternoon and everyone was outside on the block. You had your local candy house that was busy and the boys and the corner who were busy as well. On the end of my block, they sold weed and ecstasy pills. You would think that selling weed and ex pills wasn't as busy as selling rocks and blows. That shit was booming and a lot of traffic was coming thru. Right now it was slow, but as soon as the sun drops it's going down. I moved out of my parents home when I was twenty one and haven't been and don't plan on going back. Don't get me wrong I have some cool parents, but now they're heavy into going to church and you know how that goes. When I tell you that they're always preaching and quoting every scripture out of the bible so much that the two of them could start their own church.

This sudden changed happened out of the blue. One Sunday my parents went to church, joined and now they live to serve the Lord. It's nothing wrong with it because I believe in God, but I also sin like a mother fucker.

I lived in a two bedroom apartment, in a two flat building in K-Town. I know that I don't live in the best area in town, but my apartment is newly remodeled with all updated appliances. I lived on the second floor and an older couple and their teenage son lived on the second floor. We all were cool and got along with one another. I respected them and they respected me and minded their business. My landlord was strict and didn't mind me sitting on the porch, throwing parties, or having company. It was boring right now, so tonight I was ready for some action.

"What's popping tonight because it's boring as hell? I need to step out and have some fun." I said.

"Tonight it's a few parties pooping. It all depends on where you want to go. You know sometimes you be acting all bougie and shit, so we have to establish where we are going," said Emani.

"Girl I know one thing for sure and that is, ain't nobody trying to go any place where you can get shoot. You're always trying to go to the hood parties to chase behind Ty." Kamara said.

"That's so not true. It just so happens that we be in the same party at the same time. For the record, Ty is following behind me boo." Emani said.

"Yeah okay but anyway to answer your question Tichina, it's a few parties that are popping tonight. You have The Shrine, Red Kiva, KOD, Encore, & Red Diamond." Kamara said.

"I just want to look cute, party and be surrounded by a gentleman. I don't have time to be in a party with a bunch of young people." I said.

"Excuse me but we are young, well I don't know about you two, but I am. Besides Tichina you always want to party with those suit and bow tie wearing dudes. I don't care how they dress. They're all the same to me once the clothes come off." Emani said.

We all busted out laughing as we brought up the time when I met this guy in the party. He was fine, clean, nicely dressed and drove a Benz. The only problem was that he lived with his mother. When he tried to explain to me why a thirty-year old man still lived with his mother. All I could do was shake my head. He told me that all has four baby mothers had child support on him and that he couldn't afford to pay rent on his own. After that, I blocked his number and stop talking to his ass. Ladies, you have to watch out for these men. Always, always, always do a background check on every man that you meet. I was still low-key stuck on the bougie comment that Emani made. You see I'm not bougie, I just don't do hood shit. Just because I'm from the hood doesn't mean that I should act like it. Kamara and I are more similar when it comes to certain things. We are the calm ones and act more ladylike. I'm the smart one and no I'm not just saying that because it's me. Since I've been through so much I always have my antennas up and my thinking cap on. I have to think for all three of us whenever something occurs. I'm blunt and don't care for shady or disrespectful people that try to play me. Kamara was the ditzy one. When we were younger should would let men play her as if she was a toy. She's such a sweet heart, a care bear and could be easily mislead. She's keeps things inside and doesn't bother to tell anyone. That's why I always keep an eye on her. Emani was the hood one and not to be fucked with. She's like a rose from the concrete. One thing about her is that she's smart and intelligent. Emani is a good actress and cold fool many. It's always been like that, but we all loved and accepted one another for who we are. We all continued to chill out on my front porch until we became hungry. Emani offered to run to Popeye's to buy some chicken. Kamara and I both gave her some money on the chicken, making sure that she had enough. Kamara had a little girl and Emani had three children, two boys and a girl. Maybe in the future I will have a child, but right now I wasn't about that life. I was more concerned about making sure that I had myself together first before I became a mother. When I became a mother I wanted to be a wife and have a husband that loves me unconditionally. Now a days there aren't that many families any more. Everyone is so busy making and having babies here, there, and everywhere. There are more baby showers than weddings. Don't let me get started on how every girl wants to be a trap queen. If that isn't the dumbest shit that I've heard of before. There isn't anything wrong with dating a drug dealer, but I don't prefer that type of man. For one I don't have the time for everything that comes along with it such as the woman, drug cases, and jail time.

Emani made it back with the chicken and everyone gathered in my kitchen to eat. The central air was blowing making it cooler in my house. We all ate, talked and laughed, like we was one big happy family. Everything was all good until Emani's baby daddy called her. Tyrese aka Ty made my ass itch. He was one man that was not to be trusted. I don't care for him or his stinking cologne and Emani knows that I don't. It's like every time when Emani is with us it is always a problem. Kamara and I feel as if Ty doesn't like us, but Emani insists that he does. When Emani ended the call with him she looked at us. I could tell by the look on her face that she was about to ask me a question.

"Tichina can you please keep an eye on my children while I make a run for Ty? I promise that I will be right back. It shouldn't take me no more than an hour." Emani asked.

"Girl you know that I don't mind, but you better be back in an hour. You know that I have to take a nap before we go out tonight." I said.

"Thanks, be right back." Emani grabbed her Gucci purse and shades. She kissed all three of her children before hurrying out of the door. So it was just me and Kamara alone with the children. That was perfect because now the two of us could talk. Kamara has been a little quiet and distanced lately. To be honest I'm surprised to see that she made time to hang out with us this weekend. I asked my friend if everything was okay and what was going on with

18

her. Kamara told me that she thinks her man Lil Dave is cheating on her. Let me tell you about Lil Dave hot dick ass. He drives the bus for Chicago Transit Authority and is very flirtious. Let me rephrase that, he's very whoreish, but he's a good father. I don't know what Kamara seen in him. Both of them are totally opposite from one another, but they do say that opposites attract. I won't be surprised if Lil Dave is cheating on Kamara, it wouldn't be the first time. I listened to her tell me the numerous stunts that Lil Dave has pulled on her. I wasn't too quick to say anything negative so I just listened. The only thing that I told my friend was that time will tell and that the truth would be revealed. After our talk Kamara seemed to open up a little more being herself. I hated to see my best friend getting played and her heartbroken. We allowed the children to go outside and play. The older couple that lived on the first floor was sitting on the front porch and didn't mind keeping an eye on them. Kamara and I stayed inside under the air trying to figure out what I was wearing tonight. Two hours went by and Emani still hasn't been back. Kamara got a call from Lil Dave and ended up leaving. She said that she would call me when she's dressed and ready to go out. I told Emani children to come inside because it was getting late. They ate the rest of the chicken and I allowed them to go into my extra bedroom to watch television. It was now after the third hour since Emani has been gone. It was 8pm, I called Emani to see where in the hell she was at. She told me that she was finally on her way. Thirty minutes later I was awaken by the sound of my doorbell. I had drifted off to sleep shortly after I got off the phone with her. I laid her two year old daughter down next to her big brothers who were sleeping. I opened up the door and Emani came barging through my door smelling like weed mixed with the awful cologne that Ty, her boyfriend be wearing carrying shopping bags.

"I'm sorry Tichina, girl Ty had me with him for too long. I kept on trying to shake him, but you know how Ty can be." Emani was talking loud.

"Why are you so damn loud? Get your children and don't ask me to do another favor for your ass again," I said rolling my eyes.

"Girl please, how are you going to be their God mother and don't want to watch your God children? Look what I bought you."

Emani pulled out the most stunning all white and gold crystal, beaded dress. The price tag on the dress was

265.00. She also had a pair of gold red bottoms to match the dress.

"Girl you know that you didn't have to buy me this, but I'm really loving it." I stood in front of the mirror holding the dress up to my body.

"Yes I did and you're wearing that dress tonight. I have tickets for an all-white boat party on The Spirit of Chicago. So start getting ready and please don't ask me a million questions about this party. Kamara is already aware of everything because I just left her place right before I came here. I'm about to get out of here and I will see the both of you soon." Emani said.

"Okay that's cool. Let me help you carry the children to the car."

I helped Emani carry the kids to the car and buckled up their seat belts. Emani pulled off and I went back inside. It was going on nine pm so I decided to stay up and not continue my nap. I called Kamara to ask her if she knew who party that we were going to. She said that she didn't know and that Emani just brought her something to wear and told her to get ready.

Chapter 2

Kamara

I spoke with Tichina on the phone for only a minute. I couldn't even talk in peace without Lil Dave looking in my mouth. He was mad because I was outside earlier and not sitting in the house. I felt like taking my daughter outside and didn't want to sit in the house while he was at work. When I first walked through the door I knew that he was upset. I gave my daughter a bath and put her to bed. Lil Dave was in the living room watching a movie and had his phone in his hand. I knew that he was texting someone back and forth because of his text message alert that kept going off irritating me. The minute when I said something to him about it, Lil Dave became disrespectful. I brushed it off because lately I've become used to his verbal abuse. One second later he received a phone call and went to talk in the bathroom. During that time Emani popped up at my house to give me the clothes that she had bought me. Keep in mind I haven't told Lil Dave that I was going out yet. When he stepped out of the bathroom he was surprised to see Emani and me talking about our plans for tonight. After my best friend left, Lil Dave announced that he was about to make a run real quick.

"Make a run to where? Lil Dave do whatever the fuck you want. Just be back in here on time to watch Karli. I'm going out tonight." I said.

"Why are you just now telling me that you're going out? Fuck it, I'll just stay here."

Dave went in our bedroom slamming the door behind him. I took my bath and just relaxed for a while before I go off. Fifth teen minutes later I grabbed my bath towel, wrapped it around my body and went to the bedroom. When I opened the door Lil Dave was stroking his dick and was face timing another bitch.

"What the fuck! Nigga your nasty ass!" I lounged at him trying to rip his head off. Lil Dave jumped up, dropped his phone and quickly pulled his pants up. I was naked and on top of him going upside his head.

"You in here on face time getting freaky with a hoe!"

Lil Dave pushed me off of him. I managed to pick up his phone and the stupid bitch was still on the phone. She was topless with her breast exposed. A brown skinned hoe with a blond thin ass weave. A little thot ass bitch.

"Bitch who the fuck are you? Do you know that Lil Dave has a family?" I asked her.

"Don't worry about who I am. Yes I know all about you, but I don't care." The thot ass hoe said.

"That's okay hoe because when I catch up with you I'm fucking you up!"

The girl begun to laugh. "Bitch I'm not worried about you. Tell Lil Dave that I'll talk to him tomorrow," she said and hung up.

I turned around and Lil Dave was standing there looking stupid. "Baby please let me explain!"

"You don't have to explain shit! Do you Lil Dave because I'm about to do me!"

I strutted my naked ass in the kitchen with Lil Dave phone in my hand. He ran behind me trying to take his phone back from out of my hand. I went under the kitchen counter and grabbed the hammer. "You better not break my phone!" Lil Dave yelled as he tasseled with me.

"Get your nasty ass hands off of me before I hit you with this hammer!"

I placed his phone on the countertop and smashed it into pieces with the hammer. I picked up his cracked phone and threw it at his ass. "Here is your phone, good luck with calling that bitch back tonight!"

"It's cool, I have insurance and will have a new one tomorrow." Lil Dave said.

As of now I don't give a fuck about this relationship. If he wants to continue to cheat he can because starting now, I'm about to do me. I'm so sick and tired of all the bullshit. The only reason why I've forgiven him in the past for his cheating behavior was because of our daughter Karli. I was thinking about her and didn't want her to go through the same experience as me. I'm grown now and I still don't know my father. Growing up without a father fucked me up inside. It's been five long years that I've been with this hoe ass man. The only good thing that came out of our relationship was only our three year old daughter. I know one thing I was stepping out tonight. I got dressed in my all white, deep cut romper that Emani had bought me. I added a long gold chain with some gold gladiator heels. I looked in the mirror and I was killing it. My clear cocoa skin was flawless. The heels gave my short ass some height and boost up my confidence. My thick thighs was going to get all the attention that I wanted tonight. I removed my hair from off of my head and brushed my wrap down. My real hair was at least twenty inches, bouncy and jet black. My mother always told me that I looked just like my father and had long hair like him. Whoever he was I want to thank him for creating a master piece. I was dark skin, weighed a 150lbs solid in all the right places and was a midget compared to most at the height of 4'8". I've never had to wear weave a day in my life. I was blessed with thick eyebrows and long eye lashes. I was team natural, I didn't have to fake anything. After I approved my appearance I sprayed myself with perfume. I grabbed my clutch and IPhone and called Tichina to tell her that I was on my way. Before I left I went to go and check on Karli. She was sleeping and her television was still on the Disney channel. I turned off her television and gave her a kiss softly on the cheek. When I stepped into the living room Lil Dave was lying down on the couch watching television. He was upset, but I didn't give a fuck I was going out tonight. He looked away from the television and at me.

"I guess you dressed up tonight so that you could come up. I find out that you're on bullshit tonight I'm going to fuck you up Kamara. Don't go out there being a hoe."

"Don't worry I won't be a hoe like you. I've never once cheated on you or even entertained another man. I wish that I could say the same about you, but unfortunately I can't. It's always been woman after woman when it came to you. I always forgive you, but not anymore. As of now we aren't together. I'm giving you a month to find you a place to live." I said.

Lil Dave tried to talk his way out of getting put out but I wasn't trying to hear shit that he was saying. I left out the backdoor to where my car was parked. I lived on Mayfield and Lake in a small building. All of the tenants had assigned parking spaces in the back. I jumped in my Camry and drove down Lake Street to Tichina's house. I blew the horn so that she could come outside. She was riding with me it didn't make any sense for us to drive our cars separately. As soon as she got inside I turned my music down and told her what happened.

"You look friend, but let me tell you what went down. Girl I just got finished fighting with Lil Dave ass. He really just pulled some disrespectful ass shit tonight." I said.

"Thank you and you look cute as well. What the hell did Lil Dave do now?" Tichina asked.

"I walked in my room on him while he was jagging off his little dick, while he was face timing another bitch. We got into a fight and the girl was on the phone the whole time when we were fighting. She told me that she's knows about me and don't care."

"Kamara please tell me that you're lying. Who is this bitch? You know that I don't care for home wreckers."

"I don't know who she is, but I do know how the hoe looks. When I catch her it's going down! As for now Lil Dave got thirty days to get out of my place. Girl I'm finally free, single and done with the bullshit."

"I know that shit, sometimes we have to let go of whatever weighs us down. You know that I got your back. If you need me to help you out with Karli I got you." I said.

"Thank you and I know that it's going to be hard, but I have to get rid of him. I'm so tired of being in such a miserable relationship. Enough of that bullshit. Have you talked to Emani? I hope that her slow ass is ready."

"Yes I did and she claims that she's ready. Even though we already know that she's lying," said Tichina as she applied her Mac lipstick.

It didn't take long for us to get to Emani's place. She lived right off the expressway on Paulina. We made it to her house and of course she wasn't ready, so we had to go inside and wait to wait on her. That was the last thing that either one of wanted to do because her boyfriend Ty and his friends were inside. Emani yelled for us to come upstairs out of her bedroom window. We went inside, Ty and his three friends were smoking weed, drinking and playing the game. All eyes were on us, Ty thirty ass friends looked at us as if they've never been in the presence of real women. We didn't want seem rude, so we spoke and rushed up the stairs. They all spoke back never taking their eyes off of us. Ty spoke as well, but never looked away from the television. When we made it into Emani's bedroom she was trying to zip up the back of her jumpsuit.

"Help me out please. I don't want to bust the zipper." Emani said.

I helped her out as I struggled with zipping it up her back. "Did you try this on? You know that your booty has its own zip code." I finally got the zipper up her back.

Emani turned around. "Thanks, how do I look?"

"You look hot! I think that you should wear silver accessories tonight." Emani walked into her closet to pick out some shoes. Tichina and I helped her pick out some silver sandals, accessories and a silver clutch. Emani had a big closet filled with all designer clothes and shoes. I'm not trying to talk down or hate on my friend, but she got all of her things illegally. She cracked cards, cashed out on other people bank accounts and whatever else she get her hands into. Tichina and I never judged her because she's our friend and plus she always looked out for us. Honestly Ty has her doing all of that crooked shit, but that's their business. We just don't want to see her hurt, caught up and locked up behind all of this. Emani finally was finished getting dressed and we were ready to go. Before we left out of the door we all had a shot of Hennessy. I know that we aren't supposed to be drinking and driving, but hell tonight I was getting fucked up after everything that I've been through. We left out and finally made it to Navy Pier. Lucky for us the boat was still at the dock. It was a boat filled with people in all white attire. I'm not trying to sound sadity, but we were the best looking ones on the boat. A photographer snapped several pictures of us. We all smiled and posed for the camera as if we were celebrities. A bartender walked up and offered us champagne. We each took a champagne flute and sat at an empty table.

"I want to give a toast. A toast to new beginnings and to an awesome future. Putting an end to being unhappy and living your life like its golden." I said.

"To getting money, traveling, and the good life." Emani said.

"To friendship, the good times and the bad times that all three of us have shared. We've been friends through thick and thin." Tichina said.

We clinked our glasses together and sipped our champagne. We laughed as we witnessed a few dirty looks and stares from a few women. They weren't on shit, but we were used to the hate. The dee jay was doing his thing and I was feeling the music. I didn't come out tonight to sit down. I got up to dance, tonight I was celebrating my freedom. The last thing that I wanted to be was a statistic of being a single black mother, but I just can't fake being in love. One thing I've learned is that you can't make a man love you, he has to want to love you.

Chapter 3

Tichina

We were having a good time and feeling ourselves as we enjoyed the music. The boat was rocking on the water. I didn't know any of these people, so it actually felt good to be around some new faces and people. Emani obviously knew some people here because she conversed with a few. While we were dancing I noticed a gentleman looking at me. I tried not to look back and make it seem obvious that I knew that he was staring at me.

"Kamara don't look now, but the dude to your right, the brown skin one keeps on staring at me." Kamara played it off and took a look to her right. "Yes he's checking you and starting to walk this way. His friend is fine too," she said.

The group of men walked over to the three of us. Emani was the first to introduce herself. I turned around to face him, he kept his eyes on me making me feel uncomfortable.

"Hello fellas I'm Emani and these are my two friends, Kamara and Tichina."

"What's up ladies, nice to meet you? I'm Tee and these are my buddies." Tee flashed a smile exposing his perfect set of white teeth. I smiled back at his fine ass. His buddies introduced themselves, one was named Keith and the set of twins were Jay and Dee. They were all well-groomed and polite. I could tell that Tee was the leader of the group from the way he carried himself. I was drawn to him instantly, but wasn't going to show it. I was the type of woman who preferred to be chased. They invited us over to have a seat at their section and we took them up on their offer. They had a big round table in the corner that gave you a lovely view of Lake Michigan. Tee lead me by the hand as he pulled out the chair for me to sit down. Everyone took a seat and the bartenders came to the table with several lit bottles. All the other women stared from a far. The bartender flirted with the men and asked if he needed anything else. They all said no and that they were fine. I took a moment to peep Tee out, from the looks of things I could tell that he was in the streets. He had on a gold chain with a diamond cross, a pair of diamond earrings in his ear and a Rolex. His was smelling really good and I was curious about him. Tee must've read my mind because he spoke to me with the kindness words.

"Tichina I must be honest and say that the moment I saw you, my heart starting racing. Your absolutely beautiful, are you single?" Tee asked.

"Thank you and yes I am very single. Are you single? When I say single I mean no baby mothers, ex-girlfriends, side chicks or dips that you're still connected with and, or having sex with?" I asked him.

"I'm very single. No children or extra women in my life. I'm a very private person and I don't tolerate drama or non-sense in my life. I hope that answers your question. I would like to hear more about Tichina. Where are you from, your age, and what type of food do you like to eat?"

"I'm Tichina Jefferson, twenty six years old, with no children. I'm a Paralegal and work for a law firm called Johnson & Bell. I live on the Westside of Chicago and I love to eat fruit and my favorite food is seafood."

"My real name is Tavion, but everyone calls me Tee. I own a Moving & Storage Company, a Carwash, and a Cleaners. I'm thirty years old, from the Southside of Chicago. Surprisingly my favorite food is also seafood."

"Get out of here." I rolled my eyes. "You're just saying that because I said that I love seafood."

"No lie, see check this out." Tee looked away to ask his friends, who weren't paying us any attention. They were busy talking Kamara and Emani. "What's my favorite food?" Tee asked his buddies.

"Seafood." All three of them said at the same time.

"See I told you that I love seafood. Maybe one day we can go out to eat. I mean if you don't mind me taking you out."

"I would love that, but I have to keep it real with you. I not for none of the bullshit and craziness. I don't have time for the drama or your groupies." I said.

I looked past my shoulder and seen all the attention that we were getting. They act like Tee and his crew were celebrities. The last thing that I wanted to be was one of his groupies or I dated her before girl. Tee understood what I meant when I said groupies.

"Never mind them, I don't even know those people. They don't even know me. The problem is people think that they know you, when they don't have no idea who you really are. I promise you no bullshit, no drama and no games."

I listened to Tee talk and explain his lifestyle to me. From his conversation he seemed very intelligent. He spoke with conviction, like he knew what he was talking about. I felt as though that he could teach me a thing or two. Emani sent me a text message asking me if I was having a good time. I replied back yes and asked her if she was good. Emani said yes, I didn't even bother to ask Kamara if she was having a good time. I could see that she was enjoying herself, smiling really hard in Keith's face. I was happy for my friend, it was good to finally see her smiling. Tee explained to me that during the summer he throws a boat party once a month. It was something that everyone could attend. A lot of people would never get a chance to dock a boat, so he was happy to give everyone that opportunity. He seemed like a nice and considerate person on the inside if you were on his good side. I still had to watch out for him because those were the type of people that would kill you if you cross them. Tee asked if I would take a picture with him. I didn't see a problem with taking a picture with him. The photographer came over snapping plenty pictures of us. Hours later the party was over and so was the fun.

The next day while I was at work, I sat at my desk day dreaming about Tee. I've never felt this way about a man before. I imagined myself with him in the bedroom doing all types of freaky things with him. Ring! Ring! Ring! Damn, why did the phone have to ring? It was a call from within the company so I answered the phone quickly.

"Hello Johnson & Bell Law Services, how can I help you?"

"Hello Ms. Jefferson we have a delivery for you in the front. When you have time may you please come and pick it up?"

It was the receptionist calling from the front lobby. I told her no problem. I would have my packages delivered to my job because I didn't want to miss my delivery. The funny thing was that I haven't ordered anything recently. As I walked to the front I said hello to a few of my coworkers. When I made it the receptionist she greeted me with a smile.

"Hello Tichina, give me one second while I go and get your package. She stepped in the back to the smaller office and came back out with an Edible Arrangement. It was beautiful and colorful with strawberries, pineapples, green apples, and bananas. I was smiling from ear to ear and couldn't wait to get back to my desk to call Tee.

He was waiting on my call. "Hello queen, how are you doing today?" He asked me, hearing his voice made me blush on the inside and outside.

"Hello king, I'm doing fine. Thank you so much for the Edible Arrangement. I can't wait to get home to eat my fruit. How is your day going so far?" I twirled my hair waiting on his response.

"I'm doing fine. You're very welcomed. When you mentioned that you love fruit, I felt that getting you a fruit basket was the best idea."

"I see that someone was paying attention and remembered where I worked at." I smiled.

"Oh yes I pay attention and listen to what interest me. You are who I want and I'm not going to stop until I have you." Tee said.

"Time will tell Tee, let's just see how everything works out." My work phone started lighting up indicating that I had other callers. "Tee can I call you when I get off? I'm getting other callers."

"No problem queen, make sure that you give me a call when you make it home."

"Sounds great and thank you again, talk to you later."

I resumed back to my job. The phone was ringing off the chain. When I was able to step away from my desk, I placed my fruit basket in the employee refrigerator. Four more hours to go and I will be off work.

Once I made it home I showered and got comfortable. Monday's were always the busiest and leaving me drained out by the end of the day. As I started to prepare dinner I had to call Kamara and Emani on three way to tell them all about Tee. I was eager to tell them about the attention that Tee was showing giving me. They both were off work, at home and available to talk.

"Today Tee sent me a beautiful and delicious edible arrangement to my job. From the way that we were clicking at the boat party last night. I kind of felt that he liked me, but I wasn't expecting him to move so fast. He's certainly my type of man. I just pray that he isn't like all the other assholes that I've met in the past."

"That's dope! Tee seems like a pretty cool dude. Tichina that's going to be your man. Watch you wait and see," said Emani.

Kamara jumped in the conversation. "Yes I agree with Emani, he seems cool. Give him a chance and if it doesn't work out then just stop fucking with him."

"I am feeling him and I guess that I will give him a chance. The minute that I feel some shady shit going on I'm done fucking with him. From his lifestyle I know that it's someone in the cut. Tee is paid and you know what that means. More money and more problems."

"You're right about that being paid and having money part. You know that I had to do a background check on all four of them. To sum it all up they're really about their money and not to be fucked with. Word on the street is that Tee older uncles used to run the city. I also heard that Tee and Keith was single. One of the twins Jay, has a baby mother and the other twin Dee has a baby on the way." Emani was always the one to find out everything on any and everybody.

"Great he's single so I should be drama free. Ladies wish me luck, I'm going to test the water out. I will give him a chance and see where this takes me. As a matter of fact I'm about to give him a call like I promised. Thanks for the information Emani. Kamara since you are single and so is Keith are you going to talk to him?"

"Girl I've been talking to Keith all day. He asked me out on a date, so Emani I need you to babysit for me on Friday." Kamara said.

We all busted out laughing because it was strange to hear that Kamara was seeing someone else besides Lil Dave. "I

don't know why you're laughing at me. I'm serious."
Kamara said laughing.

"Girl Lil Dave is going to go crazy once he finds that you're seeing someone else. You know a man can cheat on you all the time, but that one minute that you give them a taste of their own medicine. They can't take it." Emani said.

"We should go out on a double date. I will set it up Kamara for Friday. I'll talk to you girls later. I'm about to call Tee right now."

I ended the call, but before I called Tee I finished cooking my dinner for tonight. First I wanted to make sure that I had eaten before it got too late. Tavion had to have my undivided attention. After I was done eating I picked a few pieces of fruit off my basket and began to eat them. I called Tee and he answered on the first ring.

"Hell queen, I've been waiting on your call all evening. I was starting to get concerned. I thought that maybe you didn't like me anymore." Tee started laughing, causing me to laugh.

"I love a man with a sense of humor. I was eating earlier and now I'm enjoying my fruit. What are you doing?" I asked him.

"Actually I was just lying down waiting on your call. I was busy earlier, did a little running around and now I can finally relax. I'm all yours beautiful. So Miss Tichina please tell me more about yourself. Do you have any siblings? Do you like to travel? What do you like to do for fun? What places would you like to go that you've never been to?"

That was the first time that a man actually ask me questions that I actually didn't mind answering. Usually they would ask me, what's my favorite sexual position? When can we chill? What do you like to drink? I was starting to like Tee more and more.

"I'm the only child. No sisters or brothers, but Kamara and Emani are the closest thing to my sisters. I enjoy traveling, but I haven't been on a trip in a year. For fun I enjoy bowling, skating, sky diving. I'm such a risk taker and love a thrill. The one place that I would love to visit is Hawaii, on a white sand beach."

"I haven't been to Hawaii yet, maybe one day we will go. In the meantime I will like to take you out this weekend.

Keith is feeling your friend Kamara, maybe we should all go together. Do a couple thing, if that's cool with you and your friend?" Tee paused for a minute, "Hold on Tichina I have another phone call."

"Okay." While I was on hold I starting thinking what Emani had mentioned to me. Tee had to have some major paper if he was talking about taking trips to Hawaii. He returned back on the phone. "I'm sorry about that queen, now back to what we was talking about."

"Yes we can double date this weekend. I haven't been on a date in a very long time."

"Well if you make me a part of your life there would be unlimited dates. I know that everything that I'm saying right now sounds corny. I'm not going to lie, I'm surprised at the way that I'm talking. It's something about you that I can't resist." Tee said.

The feeling was mutual, but I won't be too quick to show him how I feel. Tee and I spoke on the phone for about another hour until I fell asleep. While I was sleeping I dreamed that I was having Tee's baby.

Chapter 4

Emani

Today I was busy at work stealing as much patient's information that I could. I'm a Medical Records Clerk at Rush University Hospital. I made 16.00 dollars an hour, but with three children that wasn't enough to live off of. Especially when you enjoy the finer things in life. Only three people know what I do and that's, Tichina, Kamara, and Ty. Tyrese aka Ty and I have been on and off for five years. We have three children, Tyrese Jr. who is three years old. Tyshawn who is two years old and deaf, and my baby girl Tyesha who just turned one years old. I loved all of my children to death and would go to war for them. I hustle hard for me and mines. See I grew up in a household with several family members. My mother and I have a friend type of relationship. She was the type of mother that never wanted to grow up. My grandmother aka Big Momma had fourteen children, seven girls and seven boys. All of my aunts and uncles had children, producing a total of twenty eight. I was my mother's only child. Growing up I was in the house with all my cousins. My mother would run off for a week or two, but will always come back like everything was fine. She acted like that shit was normal and after a while it did become the norm. Thank God that I had some great family members that looked out after me. They made sure that I kept my mind on books and not on boys. I was a combination of smart and sassy. After high school I was afraid to go off to college, instead I went to school to learn a trade. Big Momma wanted me to go away, but I knew that she couldn't afford it. I enrolled in Illinois School of Health Careers for the Medical Records Technician course. I knocked that course out in a year and landed my first job here. In between time I met Ty at a house party. He was with a group of his friends and was looking good. At that time I never had a serious boyfriend and I was still a virgin. Ty approached me and ever since that day I was down for him. I just wanted to be loved. I shared my first everything with him. My first kiss, first time having sex and my first child. Ty was my world although he was a little rough around the edges. When I first met him he was an aspiring rapper trying to get out there. When that didn't work out Ty started dealing drugs and doing other things to make money. No matter what Ty did to make money he always made sure that his family was straight. Tichina and Kamara didn't like Ty. They felt that he has introduced me to a bad lifestyle and used me to make dirty money. When Ty needed me he would use me to be a part of some of his licks when business needed to be handled. He didn't force me, it was my choice to be a part of whatever he asked me to do. Not only that but that's how I was able to keep up with everything that he was doing. I know everything that Ty does to make the almighty dollar. Do I agree with it? No, but I'm his girl so I hold him down. Besides I don't trust the hoes that's working with him named Tweety and Sweetie. Sunshine was cool and the only one that I got along with. As a matter of fact I haven't heard from her in a few days, I wonder what she was up to. Ty used the girls to set up niggas throughout the city and out of state. He always told me that once he makes enough money that he's going to move me and the children out of Chicago. The money was taking too long to be made and the clock was ticking.

It was 5:30 pm and finally time for me to get off work. I couldn't wait to get home and use all my new social security numbers. Thankfully I didn't live to far from my job so it take long for me to get home. My children were already at home. The oldest two were out of summer camp and my baby girl was out of daycare. My aunt was paid $100 dollars weekly to pick up my children from summer camp and daycare and waited till I arrived home. As soon I walked in the door my children came running to me. I hugged them one by one and thanked my aunt as she ran out the door. I laughed and shook my head at her, she was always ready to go out the door when I made it home. I started dinner and pulled out my MacBook. I managed to get forty patients social security numbers. I could sale this numbers or I can use them to order me some items. I usually ordered items and sold them or ordered things for me personally. I would have all the items sent to my aunt house or purchased gift cards. An hour later dinner was done and I had purchased a few things. I cooked fried chicken, spaghetti and corn. I gathered my children at the table and fed them. While we were eating Ty came in the house from being outside all day. From the look on his face I could see that he was having a bad day. I fixed him a plate as he hugged and kissed our children. Ty was unusual quiet for some apparent reason. I paid it no mind as I hurried the children upstairs to bath them and put them to bed. Now that the two of us were alone Ty opened up and explained to me what exactly was going on.

"Remember I told you about that lick we pulled over the weekend? Ty looked at me serious as if something went wrong.

"Yes how did it go? I asked him, but Ty didn't say anything. I shoved him, "Ty what happened? Tell me something you're starting to worry me."

Ty looked at me like with a, I fucked up look upon his face. "Some foul shit went down and we had to do what we had to do."

"What exactly did you have to do?" I looked at him waiting on his answer. It was 9pm and getting late. I was prepared to get me some dick and go to bed. I wasn't expecting to be going through this. Ty turned on the television, the news was on. The words Breaking News flashed a crossed the screen. We both sat back and watch as the news reporter told the story.

"I'm standing right in front of a home in University Park where one person was found dead and another person was found critically injured. Both of the victims were both shot in the bedroom of the home. The mother of one of the victims said that she hasn't heard from her son since Saturday evening. She stated that when he didn't show up for Sunday dinner that's when she became suspicious. She then came to his home and entered with her spare key and discovered her son and his girlfriend in a pool of blood.

That's all the information that I have for now. I'm Anita Pedia reporting live from University Park."

I looked over at Ty, waiting for him to tell me what went down. "Are you fucking serious? What in the hell happened, and you better tell me everything Ty?!"

"Calm down before you wake up the children. Man, Sunshine tried to play us for that nigga! When we got there she told Duke everything and the nigga bust at Bari first hitting him in the shoulder. We did what we had to do, kill him and her, grab the cash and got the fuck out of there." Ty said.

"Damn now you have a bigger problem on your hands. Sunshine is still alive, you better pray that she dies because if she doesn't she's going to talk. Fuck!" I was angry.

"I know that's where we fucked up at. I've been keeping my ears to the street and I heard that she's in critical condition in Cook County Hospital."

I was so scared and afraid like I had did the hit. This could go wrong in two ways. Sunshine could live and tell the police everything or tell Duke people everything. Either way it was going to be some consequences if she lived. Ty wasn't in the position to go to war with nobody. Hell he didn't even have a real squad. Now he did some dumb shit and has put me and his children in a fucked up situation. I feared for our lives and something had to be done. Damn that didn't even sound like Sunshine, I can't believe that she felt for a nigga and turned on Ty. Sunshine did mention to me that Duke was getting major money and was starting trying to cuff her. I just would've never thought that she would could with the plan and not stick with it. Speaking of money, Ty never mentioned how much money that they got out of the ordeal.

"Ty how much did you get from the safe?" I asked.

"It was only thirty thousand in the safe, not one hundred and fifty thousand that Sunshine told us about. We didn't have time to search the place because we had to get out of there."

That's crazy being that they only received fifth teen thousand a piece. They were lucky that Sunshine wasn't in the picture because then they would have to split it three ways. I turned the television off, I needed it to be quiet as I started to think of a plan. With Sunshine alive that was a big problem. Ty and I and both laid in the dark as I thought of a plan.

"I have a plan." I said.

What's that?" Ty asked.

"Tomorrow I will go up to the hospital to check on Sunshine's condition. If she's conscious maybe I can persuade her not to talk by offering her some money. Normally these days some people receive a miracle and snap out of critical condition. I just need to see her for myself, you can't believe everything that the news tell you."

"I was more than sure that she was dead before we left. Damn I hope that she doesn't live, that hoe must die." Ty said nervously.

I rolled over next to him and kissed him. I know right now was not a good time to be fucking, but talking about all this bullshit made me horny. Sex was the best thing that we could do right now at this moment for enjoyment. I hopped on top of Ty's dick and rode him until we both climaxed.

The next day I got up, cooked breakfast and prepared for work. Ty was responsible for getting our children ready for summer camp, day care and dropped them off every morning. I arrived to work on time and performed my duties. Today I was quiet and reserved, all I thought about was what Ty had done. Ty didn't make me feel any better by calling my phone every hour while I was at work. I told him to stop calling to tell me about something that you heard. I wasn't trying to hear that all that shit. I was going up to the hospital to find out what I needed to know. Throughout the day I kept myself busy and eased my mind as I counted down my work hours to end.

Finally it was time for me to get off work. Cook County Hospital was right next door to my job, so I drove over and parked in their parking lot. I walked inside and by pass the front desk. My plan worked, it was easier for me to get upstairs without a visitors pass because I was wearing scrubs. I got on the elevator and got off on the ICU unit. It was pretty and chaotic on the floor. I fit right in taking my time looking for Sunshine in every room. One minute later I found Sunshine lying in bed. She didn't look at all like the beautiful, light skin, hood beauty that every man lust for. Her head was three times swollen and wrapped in soiled bloody bandages. I slowly entered her room and walked over to her. The machines that were hooked up to her body peeped causing me to become nervous. It was hard for me to look at her and not cry, they fucked her up pretty badly. Sunshine was unstable and unaware that I was there. A tear trickled down my face as I prepared to do something that I really regret, but I had to do it. Quickly I grabbed a wash cloth from off her nightstand and placed it over her nose and mouth. Moments after her machine started to beep and Sunshine flat lined. I rushed out of there and managed not to be seen. As I walked quickly down the hall several nurses all rushed to Sunshine's room. I made it to the elevator, but thought about taking the stairs instead. Running down the stairwell I heard them call the Rapid Response Team on ICU. I made it to the ground floor and before I opened the door I fixed my face and hair making sure that I didn't look guilty. I walked out of the hospital and made it to my car. Once I got inside I broke down and cried.

When I made it home Ty was there waiting on me. I was still shaken up from what I just did. Ty could see that I was a little shaken. He didn't waste any time asking me several questions. I poured myself a glass of patron and sipped it straight.

"Sunshine was fucked up, her head was huge and I think that she was missing her right eye. I took a towel and suffocated her. She died as I was doing it. She's dead bae, I took her out of her own misery." I was breathing heavily and continued to sip on my Patron.

"Did anyone see you?" Ty asked as he puffed on his Newport.

"I fit right in with all the other hospital employees because of my uniform. I went in and out very quickly that no one ever noticed me. You better be happy that I love you. I've never killed anyone in my life before, I feel unstoppable."

"I love you too baby and I promised to never put you in this position again to ever do something so foolish." Ty kissed me softly on my lips.

My cell phone rang and I see that it's Tichina calling me. "It's Tichina, should I answer?" I asked Ty.

"Yes answer your phone and talk to your friend just like you normally would."

I inhaled and exhaled before answering my phone. Tichina always call me while she was on her way home from work to chit chat. I answered and spoke with her on the phone as if I just didn't commit a murder.

Chapter 5

Tyrese

Shit was crazy last week, but it felt good that I didn't have to worry about Sunshine anymore. The suffocation killed was a success and killed Sunshine. I don't know what I would do without my baby Emani. She is a real ride or die chick that always came through for me whenever I needed her to. Since the incident I haven't spoken to Bari trigger happy ass. He got his money and probably already blew it on hoes and drugs. I had other plans in my future with my money, right now I was stacking and saving. I was in the process to meet up with Tweety and Sweetie to discuss our next lick. They met up with me at my buddy Maine place which was the spot where we normally met up at. Maine was cool as a fan, we went back since the age of 15. When I arrived I knocked on the door several times. I don't know what the fuck was going on inside, but someone better answer the fucking door.

Knock! Knock! Knock! Knock! "Who is it?" Tweety asked on the other side of the door.

"It's Ty bust this door open!"

Tweety opened the door, gave me a dirty look and rolled her eyes. Tweety was tall, brown and slim, model type chick. We liked to use her for rich white men. She had a mean attitude on her. Today I wasn't having that shit, fuck around and get the shit smacked out of her ass today. I didn't even bothering speaking to her ass. Sweetie was sitting on the couch, she got up showing me love giving me a hug. Now Sweetie was cool and a sweetie pie, her name fit her. She reminded you of the girl next door. The only thing that she lack in was knowledge. Sweetie was young, dumb and easy to manipulate. Only twenty two and very vulnerable. On her first lick we sent her off on a nigga that we were watching on Instagram. To make a long story short she got up with him and allowed him to use her. Sweetie reported back to us that he was getting money, but that was another story. When we ran up on him he had a room full of counterfeit money. Apparently he was doing all that stunting on social media with fake money. The only reason why I was upset with Sweetie, was because she withheld important information from us, such as when they went out of town and they had to run out of the restaurant because he paid the bill with fake cash. If we would've known that that nigga wasn't on shit, we would've crossed him off our list. I walked toward to the back to go holla at Maine. He was in the back handling business, cooking up some coke that we took away from some dudes up North.

"What's up Maine? I shook up with him. Maine and I were both four corner hustlers. We both got 4CH tatted on our arms when we were younger. Maine was the smart and calm one. He was also very trustworthy and my day one since A1.

"Man I'm always done, here I have three thousand for you." Maine threw the rubber band of cash at me. I took a seat down at the table across from him. I didn't bother to count the money because I trusted him. Now if it was anyone else I would've counted the money. It was business nothing personal. Maine was finishing up cooking the product. We talked for a moment in private before we started the meeting. Tweety and Sweetie were busy watching television with sad looks upon their faces. The sad looks was for the loss of Sunshine.

"Check it out tomorrow is Sunshine's funeral. I'm fucked up inside because we lost our girl. She was family, like a sister to the all of us. Sunshine will truly be missed." I didn't continue to speak too long on the subject and cut it short.

Tweety had a questioning look on her face. I dared her ass to challenge me with any questions. She gave a look that showed that she wanted to know what all went down during the set up. Her lips moved and the questions started.

"Where is Bari? Why was Sunshine shot in the face like that? What the fuck exactly went down?!"

"That's a good question I don't know where Bari is, he's supposed to be here sitting with us right now as well. Bari was shot in the shoulder, he might be somewhere recuperating."

"How do I know if that will ever happen to me? You never said getting killed was a part of the plan."

"Tweety we never know what to expect when shit goes down. In this case Sunshine and Duke was both killed."

Tweety cut me off in the middle of my sentence, not allowing me to finish what I was saying. "You were supposed to protect her!" She cried.

The whole room went silent, I allowed Tweety to vent and let it all out. Tweety was angry and upset with the wrong people. At this moment I didn't want her to feel as though we snaked Sunshine. "Look Tweety, Sunshine was killed with that nigga because she switched up on us. She didn't go down with the plan that we discussed. If anyone of you do the same you will get the same consequences. Do you understand?" I said what I had to say. It was more than a statement and not a choice.

"I want out!" Tweety jumped her skinny ass up from the chair and tried to leave out the door.

I pushed her skinny ass back down. She fell on the floor crying hysterically and shit. "Ain't no mother fucking way out bitch! Besides you still owe my money for the time when I bailed your funky ass out of jail. If you ever run your fucking mouth you will be joining Sunshine! Do you understand?!"

Tweety nodded her head up and down. My eyes gave her a killer look, she responded by saying yes. She had me fucked up if she thought that it was that easy to get out.

Sweetie watched on the sidelines with fear in her eyes. I continued the meeting by telling them that we were chilling out for a week until shit died down. I don't know if any of Duke people knew that we did it or planned on retaliating. Before I left I hollered at Maine asking him if he heard anything from Bari. Maine hasn't seen or heard from him either since the home invasion. The girls left out and I shot Sweetie a text on low telling her to keep an eye on Tweety. She gave me the word that she would. Now that Sunshine was gone I had to replace her fast. I know that it wasn't going to be hard trying to get someone that resembled her. I called Bari up, it took him a minute to answer his phone. He sounded tired and shit. I told that nigga that I was on my way to holler at him. He said that it was cool, but Bari didn't have a choice. I needed to know what he was doing for him not to reach out to anyone in a week. Bari laid his head out South in Englewood. I hated going over there because I always had to have at least three bangers on me. Those niggas from Englewood was wild and if you appeared scared, then they would pull it. As I rode threw his neighborhood niggas watched me like a hawk, throwing up GD. Bari was the only Gangster Disciples that I rolled with. He was cool because he used to fuck with one of my female cousins back in the day. We did some business together that went well and the rest was history. I pulled up in front of Bari's house that he shared with his baby mother and child. I called and told him to bust the door down before I stepped out my car. I stepped on his raggedy porch as Bari swung the door opened.

"What's up nigga? Where the hell you been for a week?" I looked around his place making sure that anyone was there but us two.

"Shit I've been lying low. I saw that shit all over the news. I've been out of sight as that shit unfolded. I heard that Duke funeral is tomorrow. Word on the street is that Duke had cameras and his people plan on retaliating.

"So what I'm not worried about them niggas. Besides we were masked up, they didn't see our faces. So we don't have shit to be worried about."

"All of that is true, but they know that Sunshine was up with everything. What if they do their homework and find out that she was working with us?" Bari puffed on his blunt. "You wanna hit this shit?"

"Nah I'm good. We're gonna be fall back and take a week off. After all this shit dies down, then we're back at it. I need to recruit another bad bitch soon to replace Sunshine."

"I think I might have someone in mind. Her name is Tootie. Man that bitch is super thick, I'm talking Buffy the Body thick. She knows a lot of niggas that get money." Bari exhaled the weed smoke in the air.

"Yeah well I'll keep her in mind, but in the meantime we have to lay low and continue to keep our ears to the street. Let me get the fuck up out of here, you know that I don't like to fuck around in Englewood. Aye, keep your phone on too nigga just in case I need to get in touch with you."

I got out of there and made it to the expressway without a problem. I wouldn't be out there again no time soon. I was aware that Duke funeral was tomorrow when Emani showed me all the love that Duke was receiving from off social media. Sunshine funeral was on Monday at Corbin's. I made a couple of more stops before I went back in the house.

Emani friends were over at the place when I arrived. I spoke to Tichina and Kamara, although they don't really care for me. I plopped down on the couch and grabbed the Xbox controller. They were in the dining room gossiping about all the killings. I listened to Emani lie and act like that she didn't have a clue as to what was going on. I turned on the game and began to play NBA 2K16 against my two sons. My baby girl was in the kitchen with her mom and friends. Thirty minutes into playing the game I wanted a beer, so I went to go grab one from the fridge walking pass the ladies. As I walked back into the living room I overheard Emani asking Tichina about her new boyfriend. Tichina smiled saying that her and her new dude was doing fine. I couldn't believe that Tichina mean, snotty ass had a boyfriend. She showed off Emani and Kamara her wrist, displaying her diamond bracelet. Apparently her new guy bought it for her. Emani and Kamara both gazed at her diamond bracelet and was happy for Tichina. I laughed at their corny asses. They all turned to look at me, that's when Emani yelled for me to get out of the kitchen. I went back in the living room to finish playing the game. Shortly after Tichina and Kamara left. Emani locked the door behind them and came to place our daughter on the couch. I kissed her on the cheek as she sat Tyeisha down. Emani scrunched up her face when I kissed her. I asked her if she was cool, she replied back with a snippy yes. I shrugged my shoulders and continued to play the game with my sons. Emani went in the kitchen to prepare dinner, she was throwing pots and pans around distracting me from the game. I went in there to see what in the hell was going on.

"What's going on baby? Do you want to talk about it?" I hugged her from behind.

"When was the last time that you bought me something?" Emani turned to face me with her lips poked out.

I had to think about the last time that I bought her something. It was maybe a month ago when I surprised her with those pair of one thousand dollar Chanel sandals that she wanted.

"Whatever you want you got it. You're my baby and I love you." I kissed her on the forehead.

"I want to go to Disney World for Christmas. Me, you and the children, on a family trip. Each of us could open up one gift there and celebrate when we come back home." Emani said.

"You got it! Book the trip!"

"Thank you!" Emani kissed me and ran into the dining room yelling, "Children we're going to Disney World for Christmas!" They all screamed in joy. Even my baby girl Tyeisha was happy and she didn't even know what Disney World was. I stood back and watched my family, they meant everything to me. I will kill and die for them.

Today was Monday and the day of Sunshine's funeral. I wasn't going, but Emani was attending. I didn't think that it was a good idea for her to attend, but she insisted on going. She said that she wanted to say her last goodbyes to Sunshine. As she was getting dressed I got a phone call from Bari. He was ready and anxious to get back out there. I told him that he had to play it smart, sit back, and wait until it was time to bust a move. If he had a problem with then he can bust a move on his own, but leave me out of that shit. The last thing that I was doing was going to jail for being too greedy. Patience was the key and I was going to take this week off as well to get my mind straight. I can't afford to lose another person or dime. Everything counted and added up at the moment. If I was going to be running in these niggas homes it had to be worth it.

Chapter 6

Emani

Corbin's Funeral Home wasn't as pack as the funeral's that
I've attended in the past. I walked inside and a funeral
assistant ask who service was I here for. "I'm here for
Natasha Smith." I politely said. He directed me to the place
that I needed to go. I sat down in the back dressed in all
black attire and rocking a pair of Prada shades. It was a few
people there, but not many. The funeral should be starting

in ten minutes. There was a picture of Sunshine on a stand next her closed casket. From the way that she looked the last time that I saw her, I knew that she was having a closed casket funeral service. More people gathered inside and the funeral begun. During service several people got up and said a few remarks. The Pastor preached and tried to turn it into a church service. I didn't like to attend church. I felt that it was all just a big ass scheme. Don't get me wrong I believed in God, but you couldn't get me to step into a church. Finally it was time for everyone to say their last goodbyes. Since I was seated in the back my row went first. I walked slowly following the woman ahead of me. When I approached Sunshine's casket placed my hand on top of it and whispered that I was sorry. I turned to hug her parents and child. I started crying and couldn't stand to be there any longer. I exited the funeral home, never looking back as I heard her mother screaming and crying for her deceased daughter. Once I made it to my car I cried like a newborn baby thinking that it could've been me lying in that coffin. I pulled off crying while I was driving on route to go home. At that moment I felt like that is where I belonged. When I walked thru the door Ty was sitting on couch playing that damn Xbox like always. He looked at me and sprung up from the couch removing my sunglasses.

"What's wrong?! What happened?! Did someone try to pull some shit with you?!" Ty went off in a rage.

"No I'm fine, I'm just fucked up about the funeral and shit. Overall I'm just fucked up about death period. I can't accept it, damn!" I said.

"I told you not to take your ass to that damn funeral. How did Sunshine look, who was all there?" Ty asked while he read Sunshine's obituary.

"We didn't get a chance to see Sunshine. Her family gave her a closed casket service. It was a few people there. I saw Tweety and Sweetie but didn't bother to speak to either one of them."

"Damn she had to be in bad shape to have a closed casket."

As Ty continued to talk about Sunshine's condition I thought about my family. I'm ashamed to say that I do not have life insurance. I searched State Farm on my IPhone so that I could get some insurance. I have to make sure that my children are covered just in case something would happen to me. I spoke with a representative making an appointment for them to come to my home next week. While I was on the phone Ty went back to playing his video game. After I ended the call he asked me who I was talking to on the phone.

"What was that phone call all about?" Ty asked, but never taking his eyes off of the video game.

"I made an appointment to get some life insurance on all of us. Seeing Sunshine like that made me realize that shit is real out here. My family needs to be covered just in case we loss someone."

"That's cool, the more the better because I already have life insurance on you and the children." Ty said nonchalant. I snatched that damn game controller out of his hands.

"You have an insurance policy on me and the children without consulting with me first?! Please tell me that I'm just hearing things!" I yelled in his face.

"Yes I do, why are you upset? I've had it for a year now. You over reacting like always."

"Don't you think that you should've discussed this with me first? Damn Ty that's some grimey shit to do behind my back! If I died today then you'll cash out on a check. How much will you gain from my death?" Ty ignored me, I popped him upside his head. "How much damn it?!" I yelled.

"Twenty thousand a piece, that's all," he said.

"That's all huh, well nigga I'm getting more on your ass. You better pray that I don't fuck around and kill you my damn self!"

I stormed off and went into my bedroom to undress. I changed into something comfortable and left out the door not saying a word to Ty shiesty ass. I decided to pay the mall a visit, retail therapy always mad me happier. My first stop was Treasures at the mall. After seeing Tichina's tennis bracelet I wanted one of my own as well. Hell Ty wasn't going to buy it for me so I might as well cop that bitch myself. I had several to choose from, taking my time to see which one that would look good on my wrist. The man at Treasures allowed me to try on several until I made up my mind on which one that I was going to purchase. The three carat diamond tennis bracelet in a prong setting looked best on my wrist.

"I'm going with this one. Ring it up please." I said.

The jeweler walked over to his register. "That will be $2,198 dollars, how would you like to pay?"

"Charge it." I handed him a bogus card.

He didn't even bother to card me. I walked out of Treasures happily with my diamond bracelet on my wrist. I hit up several different stores swiping buying me and my children everything. After I was done I grabbed a bite to eat at Chipotle ordering a burrito bowl. As I stuffed my face I called Kamara to see what she was doing. She answered her phone and was just making it home from work. I didn't want to go home yet, so I asked her if I could come over and chill for a minute. Kamara said yes, besides I wanted to talk to her and not Tichina. I can't Tichina's mouth right now, ever since that she's been with Tee all she does is brags. I didn't want to hear about her and Tee all the damn time. Ty called my phone checking on me. I told him that I'll be home later and to feed the children. He was mad but I didn't care he should've not played me behind my back. I left the mall and was heading in the direction of Kamara's house.

Kamara answered the door with Karli standing by her side. I stepped inside giving Karlie a big hug and a kiss on the cheek. I reached inside the Toys R Us bag and pulled out the life sized Doc McStuffins doll. She was so happy, Karli thanked me and ran into her room to play with doll leaving her mom and me alone. I looked over at the boxes and totes that were packed in the living room against the wall by the front door.

"What you laughing at Emani?" Kamara asked.

"Girl at Lil Dave's belongings packed at the door. Boo you wasn't playing this time I see."

"Girl I'm so damn serious now, Lil Dave ass has to go. I'm tired and fed up with his shit."

"Where is he right now?" I asked peeping over my shoulder.

"At work, he claims that he's working extra hours so that he could have the money to get his own place. For all I know is that he could be with Passion, his bitch on the side that he's been fucking with. He just better be out my place by the end of the month. What's going on with you?"

"Girl for starters I found out that Ty has an insurance policy on me and the children without my knowledge. I was so upset that I had to leave the house to clear my mind."

"I'm not surprised by any of that. You know that Ty has always been about the almighty dollar with his crooked ass."

"You're absolutely right about that. I don't know how I feel about our trust right now. If it wasn't for my children I swear that I'll put his ass out like you're doing Lil Dave."

"I got fed up with Lil Dave cheating and lying ass. Your situation is something that can be discussed and worked out. Look I see your face and I know that you don't agree with me or want to hear what I'm saying. I'm only telling you this because you're my friend. You need to go home to your family. You already know how Ty gets down, that's your man so handle his ass."

Kamara paused for a second to answer her vibrating cell phone. She smiled as she answered her phone. Whoever it was she told them that she would call them back after I left.

"Sorry about that, girl that was my new boo Keith. He is so cool and sweet, check out the new purse that he bought me." Kamara went to go get her new Chanel bag. I'm not going to lie that bitch was nice, the newest one. I complimented Kamara on her new bag. Since she was showing off new items, now was the time to show off my bracelet.

"Look at the flick of the wrist." I said sticking out my arm displaying my three carat diamond tennis bracelet.

"That's nice Emani. It looks almost like Tichina's diamond bracelet, but hers is more carats. You know the one that Tee just bought her."

"Oh really? I totally forgot all about Tichina just getting a new bracelet." I admired my wrist. "Now that I'm looking at mine, I do remember and yes it does look like hers.'

"Right." Kamara said dryly while rolling her eyes.

She knew that I was lying through my teeth and that I ran to buy me a bracelet only because Tichina had one. Hell I was jealous that my friend was rocking a four thousand dollar bracelet and mine was the cheaper version. It wasn't about that bracelet, it was more about me being jealous that her new boyfriend bought her such an expensive gift. I've been with Ty for five years and all I ever received was a ring from Treasures that was only fourteen hundred. I put on a front pretending that I was happy for both of my friends. They both lucked up some six figures niggas who could upgrade them and change their lives. Don't get me wrong they both deserved to get spoiled. I was just going to sit back and watch to see how long it lasts. I felt as though I over stayed my welcomed so I got up to leave.

"Well I guess that I'll go home now and work this shit out with Ty." I said.

Before leaving I went to Karlie's bedroom to give her a kiss and a hug. She was so busy playing and talking to her new doll. Karli thanked me and told me that she would see me later. I also gave Kamara a hug although she wasn't feeling it.

"Remember what we discussed, talk to Ty. No arguing, only discussing." Kamara warned me before I left out the door.

"Whatever you say girl. I promise that I won't argue with him."

I ran down the three flights of stairs, shortness of breath. When I sat in my car Kamara was looking out of her apartment window talking on the phone. Her thirsty ass couldn't wait for me to leave so that she could call Keith back. I wave goodbye and she gave me a fake wave and smile back as she closed her blinds. Fuck her and Tichina, I'm giving both of them bitches a break. Bitches don't know how to act when they aren't used to nice things. I took my ass home to my family. When I walked in the house I seen that Ty had cleaned up, cooked, and the children were put to bed. I walked past Ty who was still sitting in front of the game and marched upstairs in my bedroom. One by one I took all the items that I purchased away in my dresser. For the first time in my life I didn't but Ty shit. Fuck Ty, Tichina and Kamara. I'm mad at everyone right about now. I lighted my oil burner, the aroma of vanilla hit the air. Vanilla always calmed me. I ran me some bath water and undressed to soak in the tub. It was peaceful just like I prefer it, but Ty disturbed my peace when he brought his grimey ass upstairs.

He knocked on the door. Knock! Knock! Knock! I ignored the knocking and tried to continue to relax. Ty entered the bathroom and just stared at me before he spoke.

"You good now? I fed the children and put them to bed while you were out busy shopping."

"What do you want, a hand? Those are your fucking children too." I got out of the tub and continued to mumble obscenities under my breath. I thought that Ty didn't hear me, he snatched me up by the neck.

"Don't you ever disrespect me again! Do you fucking understand me?!"

"Fuck you Ty! You aren't my daddy!"

He threw me down on the floor so fast. Ty went to the closet, but I didn't see what he was doing because I was trying to get up. He walked back toward me by the time that I looked up at him it was too late.

Whack! Whack! Whack! Ty whooped me with a brown leather belt. Each whip was painful on my wet body. I cried and screamed for Ty to stop. I managed to grab the belt, but Ty was much stronger than me. "Let the belt go Emani!" We both wrestled for it until Ty released his hands from the belt and smacked me across my face so damn hard. I slid across the carpet landing on the side of the bed. I grabbed the side of my face and licked my lips tasting my blood. All I felt was hatred inside of my heart. Ty never in his life has laid a hand on me before. I felt as if I was fucking the enemy. I took that ass whopping that night because I didn't have any more energy. Things will never be the same after this moment. I laid on the floor crying my heart it. Ty left me crying on the floor and left out of the room. Five minutes later I heard the front door slam. I used the little strength that I still had remaining in me and got up to throw on a one of Ty's tee shirts. I limped down the stairs and opened up my front door.

"Ty!!!!!" I yelled. Ty pulled off and zoomed down the street.

Chapter 7

Kamara

I was so happy when Emani hating ass left my damn house. I can't believe that she was that envious to go out and buy a damn bracelet. I was very close to putting her ass out of my house that I think she felt it in the air and exited herself. As soon as she left I called Keith, my new boo back quickly. I didn't stay on the phone with him but for five minutes to tell him that I would call him back after I put Karli to bed. I was really feeling him and that was different for me because Lil Dave has been the only man that I've been with. Speaking of the devil I haven't heard from him in hours. He could be with Passion, hell I was hoping that she would let him stay with her. Just being around Lil Dave made my skin crawl. I worked an half a day today because I had a doctor appointment. After catching Lil Dave up I had to see the doctor as soon as possible. Lil Dave and I haven't used in a condom in years. Although he told me that he used them with Passion, but I can't trust his word and had to get my safe checked out. His freaky, hoe ass was nasty when it came to the bedroom. I know for a fact that him and his side bitch Passion was getting down in the bedroom. Just the small glimpse that I got of her, she looked like she had several sexual transmitted diseases. He just better pray that I don't have any fucking diseases. The doctor said that I would receive all my results back in three days. I cooked and fed Karli, she is such a picky eater. I made tacos and Karli didn't want anything on them except cheese. She told me that my tacos were so good that I didn't need all that nasty stuff, only cheese was just fine. I made her promise me that one day she would try a taco with all the toppings. Too grown for her age, she promised me that she would and told me that she was full and tired from playing with her new doll. I bath Karli and then put her to bed. Now that I was free and able to talk I called Keith back.

"Hey Mr. How are you? I was smiling so hard as if he could see me through the phone.

"I'm fine, busy counting money and thinking about you. You cool over there, did you put your daughter to bed?"

"Yes, I'm cool. I've been thinking about you as well. I love my new purse, all day today every woman has been telling me that they love my purse. Even my Caucasian doctor tried to take it from me. Thank you for the gift."

"You're welcome beautiful. While I was out shopping I thought about you and decided to grab you something. The first thing that came to mind was a purse, you know it's plenty more of from where that came from. So is it safe to say that you're feeling me?"

"Just a little bit, just because you bought me a bag it doesn't mean that I should be your girl.' I giggled and said.

We both laughed and continued to talk. Keith liked to talk about himself, but not in a cocky. To me he was confident in himself and I learned a lot by listening to a person. The conversation was flowing like a river. I found out everything that I needed to know such as his birthday, about his parents, and if he's been tested for HIV. Keith flipped the script on me, asking what was me and my baby father situation. I kept it real with him and told him truth. After that Keith paused making me nervous.

"Sounds like you're dealing with a serious situation. I hope that your daughter is affected by the sudden change."
"I hope that she isn't either, that's my biggest concern. I

will have a talk with her about everything and pray that she understands."

"Yeah that's deep, but you'll be fine. Shorty, excuse me I mean Kamara I'm not trying to put any pressure on you. At the same time I don't want to step on another man's toes either. When you're ready to get up I'm just a phone call away. Right now you have your hands full."

"You're right, I can't do nothing but respect that. Right now it is totally crazy around here. That still doesn't mean that we can't be friends."

"We cool, I'm not giving up. I just need to make sure that dude is out of your system as far as romantically. I know that he's always going to be in your life because you two have a daughter. I don't want to be caught in a love triangle and have to smoke your baby father. Not that I plan to, but I'm just saying. I do hope that we can go on our date this weekend, like I said I'm not giving up. I like your chocolate ass."

"I like you as well and I'm looking forward to our date."

Damn every word that this man was saying was turning me on. Unfortunately that feeling was cut short because Lil Dave walked his hoe ass through the door. I told Keith that

I would call him tomorrow and blew him a kiss through the phone. He liked when I did that, he told me to call him first thing in the morning. I could hear Lil Dave go in the bathroom, he was talking loudly on the phone so that I could hear his conversation. Lil Dave was aware that I was awake because I had the bedroom light on. He was talking on the phone carrying on a very sexual conversation, telling Passion what he had planned for her the next time when they meet again. Lil Dave was so disrespectful and childish. I got up out of the bed to turn my light off. I bet you thought that I was going to go check him, but instead I laid back down to go to bed. I then heard him walk into the kitchen. I know that he was looking for something to eat. Out of spite I made sure that I made only enough tacos for Kamara and I. Suddenly Lil Dave barge into my bedroom amped up.

"Damn so you couldn't save me any tacos? You selfish as fuck Kamara."

"Dave you should've ate where you was at. Tell your little girlfriend Passion to make you some tacos, because I don't fuck with you like that anymore. You're lucky that I'm allowing you to stay here in the first place."

"That's why I'm fucking with Passion, she cooks and fucks me better than you. I can't wait to get out this bitch. I hate that I ever had a child with your stupid ass."

Lil Dave walked out my room slamming the door behind him. Apart of me wanted to get up and knock his ass out, but I wasn't going to behave like a fool with my daughter in the house like the last time. Karli doesn't deserve to be exposed to such behavior. Instead I went to bed because I had to be at work in the morning.

My alarm clock went off at 6:30 a.m. I got up, cooked breakfast, and prepared Karli for summer camp. Lil Dave had left already for work. That was usually because he doesn't leave out this early and starts work at 10 a.m. We left out the door. I made it to Karli's summer camp at 7:40 a.m. and proceeded to work. I'm a bank teller at Chase Bank, I've been working there for three years. The branch that I worked at was in Berwyn, right off Roosevelt. It was the first of the month and pretty busy this morning. We received a lot of business from the people in the neighborhood and the employees who worked at the mall down the street. By the afternoon it had finally slowed down quite a bit. I only had two people in my line. The

Hispanic woman who I was serving and a young black woman behind her. I spoke Spanish fluently, so serving customers who didn't understand English wasn't a problem for me. After I was done serving her the black woman stepped up next. She appeared to have a nasty attitude, with her frowned up face and body posture. She looked very familiar to me, but I couldn't pin point where I recognized her from.

"Hello welcome to Chase, how can I help you?" I politely asked her with a smile upon my face.

"I need to withdraw some money from my savings account." She had such venom in her voice and practically forced her driver license and deposit slip under my glass. Her driver license read Chiquita Jenkins. She wanted to withdraw $1600 from her savings account. As I pulled up her account, Chiquita talked on the phone to someone.

"I'm so happy that my man and I are finally going to move together. You know how much that I love me some Dave."

At first I wasn't interested in her conversation until I heard her mention the name Dave. That caught my attention, she continued to talk.

"Girl he left that bitch Kamara. She wasn't treating him right so he had to get up with a real woman." Chiquita looked at me rolling her eyes.

That's when everything was starting to make sense. Chiquita was aka Passion, the hoe had the audacity to come up to my job. I counted the bills in front of her, gave back her I.D., and her money. I wasn't going to act a fool while I was at work and risked losing my job.

"Thank you and have a nice day Passion." I said with a fake ass smile upon my face.

"I will do bitch." Passion ignorant ass left out of the bank laughing.

If she thought that she was getting the last laugh, she better think again. That was a bold move of her to pull coming up to my job. It wasn't a smart move because I printed out her account information and retrieved it for later. Today I was going to be even bolder when I got off work.

Finally it was time for me to clock out. I said goodbye to my coworkers as I left work. As I drove to go pick up my princess from summer camp, I called Tichina and Emani to tell them that we needed to meet up at Emani's place. I was on edge about that bitch disrespecting me, but I had to remain calm until I made it to Emani's place. Karli was hungry so I stopped off at Wendy's to grab us both a bite to eat. Karli was so smart, as I was driving in the direction of Emani's house, she knew where we was going. When I arrived Tichina and Emani was sitting on the porch waiting on me. I allowed Karli to go inside the house to play the game, so that she could give me some privacy.

"What's going on Kamara?" Both Tichina and Emani asked me.

"Check it out, you wouldn't believe that bitch Passion came up to my job today. She came up there to fuck with me. Talking on the phone to someone telling them that her and Lil Dave about to move together, and a whole lot of other bullshit. I printed out the bitch account information though. I'm about to go and beat the shit out of her ass. She disrespected me and I'm not going to ever let that shit ride." I passed them the paper with her account information on it.

"She lives at 3809 West Gladys, that's right off Hamlin, by the park." Emani said as she looked at the paper.

"When you want to do it?" Tichina asked, she was down for whatever.

"Right mother fucking now! I popped my trunk, kicked off my heels and changed into my sneakers.

We all got inside my car, taking the street instead. We rode up Jackson Blvd, she lived closed by Garfield Park. We pulled up on her block and parked in front of 3809 West Gladys. It was a group of young girls jumping rope two houses down. 3809 was a two flat brownstone building, with raggedy blinds hanging in the window. Me, Tichina, and Emani got outside of the car and ran up the stairs. I rang the doorbell hoping that it worked, after a second I banged on the cheap ass door. The blinds moved, someone looked out the window. The door swung open, the smell of fried chicken hit my nose. Passion stepped into the hallway with a fork in her hand.

"Bitch what are you doing at my house? If you looking for Lil Dave, you could find you some business. He doesn't want your boring ass!" Passion was tough as hell standing on her property.

I didn't say anything, instead I punched that whore in her mouth. We dragged her out of the doorway, punching and stomping her. Passion stabbed me with the fork in my shoulder. She tried to stab me in my face but missed. I grabbed the fork and stabbed that bitch in her face several times. Passion blocked her face with her arms knocking the fork out of my hands. She begun to scream and yell for help. Lil Dave stepped out on the porch like he was superman, ready to save his thot.

"Chill out Kamara! Chill the fuck out!" Lil Dave pulled Passion apart from us. Passion ran into her house crying.

"You over here with this bitch!" I stole off Lil Dave. A crowd grew around us, watching everything go down. "You foul for coming over here in the first fucking place!" Lil Dave yelled.

"Foul for coming over here, when that bitch had the nerve to come up to my job! How in the fuck does she know where I work at Lil Dave?! Huh?! It's because your trifling ass told her!" I smacked Lil Dave across the face. He lifted his hand up prepared to smack me. That's when Tichina, Emani and I jumped him. Lil Dave couldn't handle the three of us. Out of nowhere Passion came back on the porch with a gun.

"She has a gun!" Someone from the crowd yelled. Everyone ran off down the street.

"Get the fuck off of my man!" Passion pointed the gun at us. We backed away from Lil Dave slowly. I wanted to say something, but Emani stopped me, pulling my arm so that we can leave. All three of us ran and jumped in my car with Tichina behind the wheel speeding off. I was still hyped and ready for war.

"Wait a minute, back up, wasn't that Lil Dave's car back there?" Tichina backed up two cars down and Lil Dave's white Impala was parked on Springfield. I told Tichina to pop my trunk so that I could grab my steel bat out of it. I busted all of his windows out, his tail lights, and beat his car relentlessly. After taking all my anger out on his car, I jumped back in the car and Tichina drove off. I cried my poor heart out in front of my two best friends. I was hurt and fucked up inside because the only man that I've loved in my life had turned on me. Tichina and Emani told me that it was going to alright and to let it all out. "Please can we go straight to my house?" I asked the both of them. "No problem." Tichina said riding to my home. She parked my car in the back and locked the gate. When I made it in the house, with the help of them we threw all of Lil Dave things over the banister. I took them out of the back yard and placed them in the alley. Lil Dave had the nerve to facetime call me while we were in the alley.

"Nigga you got me fucked up! You shit on me after all these years over a dusty bitch. Since you where you want to be stay there and don't ever come back here. As a matter of fact you can start all over with everything!"

I took a match and lit his shit on fire. Lil Dave was on the phone screen mad as hell, calling me bitches and shit with Passion in the background."

"It's cool bitch, I'll buy him some new clothes. Money ain't a thing over here." Passion said and ended the facetime call.

"Emani lets take all of that hoe money and fuck up her life. Here is the hoe bank account information right here." I handed Emani the paperwork.

"I'm down and got you covered boo." Emani took the papers and placed them in her purse. "Right now you need to call your landlord to have your locks changed."

We all sat on the couch as I called my landlord and asked him to change my locks. I had to pay a fifty dollars to have my locks changed. It was fine I had the money and he was sending someone over in an hour. As we sat in the living room we heard the fire truck pull up in the back of the building. They sprayed water on Lil Dave's items putting out the fire. We hid in the house because I didn't want to get fined for starting a fire. They left after they couldn't get an answer out of anyone in regards of who started the fire. We all laughed about Lil Dave's shit being burned, but I was still hurting inside. I had to let it all out and just balled up in a fetal positon crying. I was thankful to have my friends in my life. Emani called Ty and asked him to bring Karli to my house and us something to eat. I took a shower and stayed in the bathroom for a very long time just thinking. Tichina would check in on my every five minutes. Trust me that nigga wasn't worth me hurting or trying to kill myself. When I heard Karli's voice I snapped back to reality and came out the bathroom. Karli was happy to see me, showing off the fake tattoo that she had on her arm. Ty bought us some Coleman's Barbecue, chicken wings and rib tips. Emani left to go home with Ty and gave me a hug.

"Thank you for always having my back Emani." I hugged her back.

"Girl you don't have to thank me. You know that we go way back since hopscotch, double dutch, and penny candy." She laughed and gave Tichina a hug as well.

Tichina stayed with me until the locksmith came to change my locks. The three of us, me, Karli, and Tichina were eating when the locksmith knocked on the door. It didn't take long for him to change the locks. Tee was coming to get Tichina to take her home. Karli was getting tired so she gave her a bath and just let me rest. Thirty minutes later Tee had arrived to come get Tichina and I asked her to place Karli in bed with me. She gave me a hug and told me to call her if I need anything. I locked the door behind her and got back in bed with my daughter. Lil Dave was calling me all night non-stop. I blocked his number so that he could stop calling. I laid next to my daughter, watching her as she slept. I know that she was going to be asking questions about her father absence, so I might as well prepare for it. My phone rang, it was Keith calling. I answered because I needed a male to talk to right now.

"What's up beautiful? I've been calling you all day, is everything cool?" Keith asked.

"No, it's not cool." I cried on the phone.

"What's wrong Kamara? Why are you crying? Do you need my help?"

I told Keith what happened in between the tears.

Chapter 8

Tichina

Among all the crazy drama that's been going on, Tee and I have been seeing one another more than often. He's been spending a lot of time at my place. We've really gotten close, don't worry I still haven't slept with him yet, although he really is hard to resist. For once in my life I was falling in love with. Something that I thought would never happen. To be honest I don't know how he deals with my stubborn ass, but he's able to handle me unlike any other man. Tee invite me to his grandmother house tomorrow. I was down to meet his family, especially his grandmother he always spoke very highly about her. Today I was going to the beauty shop to handle my wig so that I can look wonderful when I make my appearance. My hairstylist was Heaven, she had hands that were truly blessed by the Gods. No seriously her real name was Heaven and she was cold when it came to doing hair and makeup. Her salon was located on the Southside, in Englewood. I had to be there at 8am, early as hell. The earlier the better because Heaven was always crazy busy, besides I prefer to get in and out. On the way there I spoke to Kamara on the phone making sure that she that she and Karli was cool. I promise her that I will stop by there to check on them. I swear if something ever happens to my best friend, I will lose my mind. The traffic was starting to piss me off, they were always doing construction in Chicago. After fighting threw traffic, I finally made it to the beauty shop. Heaven was styling a client hair, so I sat down and waited for my turn.

"Hey Heaven, what's up." I said.

"Hey boo, you're next give me thirty minutes." Heaven said as she curled the woman hair.

I was fine with that. The beauty shop was pretty busy and backed. It was five stylist and every seat was filled. All the clients were scattered around, sitting watching television, the stylists, or talking among one another. I pulled out my book, Blackbone to read, it's by a local author from the westside of Chicago name Caryn Lee. The book was pretty good and exciting, I was almost finished. As I was reading I received a phone call from Tee. I told him that I was in his next of the woods and he said that he wanted to swing by. That was cool so I waited, because I know that it was going to take Heaven longer than thirty minutes. Ten minutes later Tee pulled up in front of the shop in his black Maserati. Everyone looked out the window as he parked, a few women whispered and looked me up and down. I told Heaven that I was stepping out in the front for a minute. Tee stood by his car waiting on me. I gave him a big hug and he didn't want to let me go.

"Check you out, you have really long hair. Why do you wear weave?" Tee pulled on my ponytail.

"I wear weave because it's convenient. I'm happy that you stopped up here to see me."

"You're in my neck of the woods. Who does your hair?"

"Heaven does my hair. Why did you ever talk to any of the stylist that work here?" I looked him in his eyes to see if he was going to lie.

"No, I just know them. Heaven my buddy, she used to talk to Justin."

"Oh okay, because I don't want to go back in there looking stupid." I rolled my eyes.

"Don't ever worry about that. Call me when you're done, maybe we could grab a bite to eat after you're done." Tee grabbed my waist pulling me closer to him. He kissed me on the forehead.

"Cool, I'll hit you up. Be safe out here bae." I walked off switching real hard. I could see Tee reflection in the beauty shop mirror. He was watching my ass with a smile on his face.

I turned around, "Creep." I said and walked back into the salon.

When I walked back inside Heaven was just finishing up her client. Two sets of eyes were glued on me. It was two women, a stylist and her client, the client was dark skin and the stylist was brown. The client was mugging me hard like she wanted to fight or something. I ignored them and took a seat in Heaven's chair. She didn't waste any time telling me that she used to talk to the twin Justin. I told her that Tee ran that by me. She asked me how did I meet Tee and said that he was cool. I told her how we met and pretty much ended the conversation, it was too many ears around in the shop. Plus the dark skin woman was all in my mouth. Heaven permed my hair and received a phone call. Whoever it was she simply no problem and ended the phone call. Fifth teen minutes later my head was on fire, it was time to wash out the perm. As we walked to the shampoo bowl, I passed by both of the women. The dark skin one said something under her breath and they both giggled like high school girls. I ignored them and took a seat in the chair. She started a conversation talking loudly about Tee.

"Tee have a different girl every day of the week. She won't last long because he always runs back to me." The dark woman said that was getting her hair done.

The stylist laughed and cosigned for her. "Girl everybody know that's your bae."

I waited patiently until Heaven was finished washing my hair. She read the look on my face. "Please just ignore them, they're hating Tichina."

"Girl you know me better than that." I got up and walked off before Heaven could wrap the towel around my head.

I stopped in front of them both. "If you have something to say to be a woman about it and keep it to yourself, because I don't care to hear the bullshit." She looked shocked and didn't say shit else.

Everyone in the shop looked over at us waiting for something to pop off. I wasn't on that, but if necessary I don't mind fucking a bitch up. I sat down in the chair while Heaven pulled out the blow dryer. She started blow drying my hair, from the corner of my eye I could see both of them talking but I couldn't hear them. One thing about me is that I don't do any talking or throw half ass shots. Ole girl sat her ass in that chair and didn't say another word about Tee. An hour went by and her stylist was finished with her hair. I'm not going to lie it was cute, but not better than my stylist. She walked passed me toward the door to exit, but before she left out she had to have the last word.

"Look you don't have to be concerned about Tee and I, because I'm that bitch that gets up with him whenever the fuck I feel like it. The woman that you need to be worried about is Kenya, she has him wrapped around her finger." The woman left out of the shop.

I rolled my eyes and remained in my seat, not allowing that to move me. By the end of my hair appointment I had gathered up as much information about the raggedy bitch. Her name was Tootie, she was 42 years old, and still out here being a hoe. Finally Heaven was finished, when it was time for me to pay her she wouldn't take my money.

"Tichina, Tee said that he got me, so put your money back in your pocket." I looked at her with trying to figure out when, what, and how.

"He called up here silly, shortly after he pulled off while I was perming your hair." Heaven laughed.

I tipped her anyway giving her twenty dollars. My hair was too cute, soft and lightly curled. I scheduled my next appointment and left out to meet up with Tee.

Tee was waiting for me at Capital Grill to have lunch downtown. I didn't bother to tell him about the incident that occurred in the beauty shop. I arrived at the restaurant with an empty stomach and curious to know about Tootie and the other woman who she mentioned was Kenya. I hugged and kissed Tee lightly on the lips. He could sense that something was wrong right away.

"Your hair looks nice, what's going on? You look like as though someone pissed you off." Tee looked at me with a serious face.

You know I'm not the one to beat around the bush so I went straight in.

"Today in the beauty shop after you pulled off some dark skinned chick in the shop by the name of Tootie brought your name up. Is that your old chick or something Tee?" I was waiting to bring up the other woman name. First I had to hear what he was going to say about this one.

"Tootie is someone who I used to fool around with back in the day. That's old news, you don't have to worry about her."

"When was the last time you fucked with her? Please tell the truth Tee."

"Right before I met you, but that shit been over with. I haven't fucked Tootie in about a month. She's just mad and hating because I'm not fucking with her ass anymore."

"Yes she's definitely mad, so mad that she warned me about Kenya. Who in the hell is Kenya and why does she have you wrapped around her finger?"

Tee became upset and started going off. Some people turned to look at us trying to see what was going on. I told him to calm down before we get put out. Apparently I pushed a button when I asked him about both women. Now I was beginning to have second thoughts about Tee and I. I wasn't going to bail out on him without an explanation, after all I'm really feeling him. I'd be a fool to think that it wasn't any other women that Tee could be entertaining.

"Look Tichina can we please enjoy lunch and I promise to tell you about everything after that."

"Well if it's going to make you so upset to the point that you embarrass me, I think that would be a good idea."

I skimmed over the menu to see what I wanted to eat. The waiter came to our table and we both placed our orders. My stomach was growling so I ate the bread and butter until our food came. Tee changed the subject and begin to talk about him and I. He could tell that I didn't want to hear anything that he was talking about. When our food came, I ate it quickly and was ready to go. I didn't care how childish and petty I was acting like right now. Tee paid for the food and we left. He followed me home as I took Lake Street straight down trying to avoid the horrendous traffic on the expressway. When I got inside I checked my hair to make sure that my curls didn't drop to bad. Tee made himself at comfortable sitting next to me on the couch.

"Tee why are you acting as if you're on trial or something? Now is the time to let everything all out."

"Kenya is my ex-girlfriend, she did some time for me and is on her way home. We're not together anymore because she's salty with me about some things. During her incarceration we both decided to go our separate ways, but were still good friends."

"On her way home? When is she getting out? Good friends like what? I need you to give me more details, before you lose me."

"She gets out next month Tichina. You have nothing to worry about. We will never get back together, never. She's good people and I promise to look out for her once she was released. As far as she and I being together that's never going to happen again. After four years people change and move on."

"I'm going to take your word and trust you. What's up with Tootie bitch? You need to check her ass Tee because the next time she tries to pull some more bullshit, I'm tapping that ass!"

I'll handle her and I promise that you don't have to worry about her anymore. You still down with me and coming to my granny house tomorrow?" Tee gave me a look that I couldn't resist.

"Yes I'm still going, why would I allow something so petty to stop me. I believe what you told, but for now on I don't want to hear nothing about you from anyone else. Since you're here let's get everything out in the opening. I want to build a relationship starting off with truths and not lies. Are you sure that you don't mess with Tootie anymore? She mentioned that she can have you whenever she wants. From looking at her, I'm not going to lie her body is banging."

"I'm done fucking with Tootie ass, she talks too damn much and likes to keep up trouble. Tootie and I was never in an exclusive relationship. She wasn't never my girl, never met my family, never been to my home. I took her out of town a few times and that's about it. Tootie was just a fun girl who I called when I was ready to have some fun during my lonely times. It takes more than a fat ass to make me fall in love with you."

Tee assured me that Tootie wasn't going to get out of line anymore and that I didn't have to worry about Kenya.

Normally when drama hits the fan when I'm dating a man I usually don't stick around to get hurt. For some apparent reason I wasn't feeling as though Tee was out to hurt me. The very first time I was following my heart and allowing it to lead the way. If I had to knock a few of his old hoes out of the way then so be it.

Chapter 9

Tee

You see one thing that I don't tolerate is a person that runs their mouth about me. Especially a mother fucker who was close to me. The twins, Jay and Dee hit my line to discuss some business. I hollered at them and told them that I would meet up with them shortly. Maneuvering through traffic and blasting Future, I watched all of my mirrors. I kept that pole on me just in case a stupid nigga wanted to try and pull it. My third phone vibrated on the arm rest. It was Tootie blowing a nigga up about nonsense. She knows that I might've heard about the stunt that she pulled up at the beauty shop earlier.

Tootie: I miss u daddy. When r u coming to see me?

Me: ASAP

Tootie: I'll be waiting on ya □□□

I played along with the silly bitch as I made my way over to One East Delaware Apartments to her place. Twenty minutes later I pulled into her underground parking lot. I called Tootie, she quickly answered her phone. I told her that I was on the elevator and to get ready to bust that door down. Tootie was waiting for me wearing my favorite color red. Her smooth mocha skin and phat ass looked good in that red bra and thong set. It was hard for me to resist her, but she had to be taught a lesson.

"Hey bae, I'm so happy to see you. I miss you so damn much." Tootie wrapped her arms around me.

I pushed her off of me. "Get the hell off of me." Smack! "What did I tell you about running your fucking mouth all the time?" Smack! Smack!

"I'm sorry Tee. I saw you and her and immediately became jealous." Tootie cried, holding her lip. "Who the fuck is that bitch anyway? Tee why do you always have to put other women before me when I've been nothing but good to you?"

"Don't worry about who the fuck she is. That's your problem, you're always worried about the next woman instead of worrying about yourself. You may have been able to get in Kenya's ear, but I won't let you fuck this one up for me." I started to walk out the door.

"Please Tee I'm sorry. Let me make it up to you." Tootie dropped to her knees, pulling out my big dick. She didn't waste any time sucking and slopping on it. I grabbed the back of her neck and roughly forced my dick down her throat. Tootie gagged as tears tricked down the side of her face. She sucked on my dick with a busted lip like the dick sucking pro that she was. Moments later I was ready to nut. I didn't pull out, hoes like Tootie I made swallow my nut because I didn't want to pop them off. I'd rather shoot down their throat instead of inside of them. I filled her big mouth with my dick and exploded. Tootie swallowed and licked all of my nut off my dick. I walked to her bathroom to grab a wash cloth and cleaned off my dick. She walked up behind placing her hand on my shoulders. We both looked in the mirror at one another, Tootie was a beautiful woman on the outside, but on the inside she was wicked. She is much older and knows better than to run off at the mouth.

"We cool bae? I promise not ever run my mouth again." Tootie kissed the left side of my neck.

"You need to find you a new beautician to do your hair. My girl doesn't need to see you the next time when she goes to get her hair done."

"Are you serious Tee?! NeNe has been doing my hair for years. I'm not going to stop going to her just because your little girlfriend has a problem with seeing me." Tootie was upset and frowned up.

I grabbed her face. "You're the messy mother fucker that had to start some bullshit. Like I said, find someone else to do your fucking hair Tootie. Do you understand me?!" I took a huge amount of her weave and pulled the side of her head.

"Stop Tee, you're fucking up my hair." Tootie begged. I released her weave and left out her door. "When am I going to see you again? Tootie asked me.

"I'll call you whenever I'm ready to fuck with you." I smiled and bounced out of there. Tootie stood at door crying a river. She knew that I was done fucking with her ass because she ran off at the mouth. I've given her too many chances I the past every time that she has fucked up. Here's thing with Tootie and I. I've been dealing with Tootie for many years, ever since the beginning. She was older than me and had her own crib and allowed me to do my thing at her place. At first it was just business, but it became personal when she whipped that head and pussy on me. I was twenty one and she was twenty eight at the time.

Tootie and I was alone during the day while her children were in school. It was a cold day in December, Tootie was in the shower and I had to take a piss really bad. I knocked on the bathroom door asking her how much longer she was going to be in there because I had to piss. She told me to come in and take a piss. I didn't mind so I stepped inside and pulled out my dick and let it out. Tootie took a peek from behind the shower curtain and looked at my dick.

"Damn Tee you hanging to be a young boy, nice." She licked her lips.

"Don't let my age fool you. I'm working with a monster." I smiled, zipped up my pants, washed my hands and walked out the bathroom.

I resumed back at the table, bagging up my work as I waited for the rest of the crew to come through. Moments later Tootie strolled out of the bathroom with a purple towel wrapped around her body.

"I want to find out what that monster feel like." She gripped my dick through my jeans and led me to the couch. At this point I've never been with any woman older than me, but that wasn't going to stop me from fucking her. When Tootie dropped that towel I was like damn. Tootie was thick like a brick and had an ass that you couldn't

110

deny. My dick grew hard, the only thing that I was thinking about was how does that pussy feel? In a matter of seconds I was naked and had Tottie bent over the couch, fucking the shit out of her. Her pussy was good, nice, tight and made me nut in ten minutes. I was embarrassed, but Tootie made me feel good and sucked my dick again until I came nutted again. She gargled my nut and then swallowed it down. From that day I was hooked. Tootie and I started creeping and fucking behind everyone back. I looked out for her when the money started flowing in like crazy. She started growing feelings and started getting clingy and shit. Tootie was with random niggas at the time and so was I with random girls, so our time together was our time together and that was all. When I became serious with this one girl in particular and brought her around Tootie she acted a fool and became jealous. That relationship didn't last long, but I still continued to fuck Tootie on the side. On my twenty ninth birthday I met Kenya. She came to my birthday dinner with twin baby momma. Although I had a date with me I was still checking out Kenya. She was beautiful and possessed an around the way girl type of attitude. I always like a woman who's laid back and not uppity. At the time Kenya didn't have any idea that I was interested in her. When twin tried to set it up between his baby momma,

Kenya shot me down. I could understand why, because she wasn't cool with playing second. After much work and sacrificing a few of my hoes on the side I managed to pursue Kenya. Things were good in the beginning until Tootie found out about her. I tried my best to separate the two, but the south side of Chicago was so small. I never stopped fucking Tootie so when she had the chance to get inside of Kenya's head all shit went crazy. I was falling in love with Kenya so I ended it with Tootie. At times when Kenya and I will fallout about petty things. I found myself back dealing with Tootie and keeping her around. My heart was with Kenya and couldn't no woman come between that. One day the feds came and broke us up. They raided our place and found drugs and cash inside. At the time I wasn't there I was out of town handling some business. By the apartment being in her name she went down for everything, but never talked. Kenya bond was denied and she was sentence to three years. That broke us apart and separated us. Kenya was officially done fucking with me for good. I've put that girl through so much pain that it was only right to give her peace. After fighting to win her back after the second year that she served I gave up. I was exhausted and the situation was draining the shit out of me. I still held her down and was going to look out for her once she's released. As far as Tootie and I that shit is dead. Now that I've met Tichina I wasn't going to allow Tootie to get in her head like she did the other females in my past. As I grew older I realize that you girl shouldn't have to deal with so much bullshit she don't deserve. This time around if Tichina was going to be the woman in my life then I wasn't going to fuck up like I did in the past. I'm older now and ready to settle down and have some children. Marriage is also in the plans, but first I had to cut off Tootie. She made it a lot easier by running her mouth which led to cutting herself off. It was time for Tootie to stop dreaming, wake up and realize that she and I will never be in relationship. Throughout all those years she may have gotten older, but still haven't grown up. She was still doing the same things and behaving the same way as ten years ago. Keeping up drama, fighting women over men, sleeping with different men, and always everywhere on the scene. Don't no man want a woman who is turning up everywhere with everyone.

Two hours later I was over at one of the twins place. Jay and I was discussing business while we waited for Dee and

Keith to join us. These were my brothers for life. I grew up with these niggas in Englewood. We used to rip and run the streets back in the day while making money. We made a pledge to make enough money and remove our families the hell out of the hood. At the age of twenty one things changed for all of us. Sixteen years later we were at the top of the game. We were trendsetters and made a name for ourselves. Nobody never fucked with us, of course in the beginning we had a few that tried to pull it, but they never got out alive. In the game you had to be about that life and a lot of these niggas was faking it out here. When the people came knocking, only the weak would get to talking. No one was not to be trusted. That's why my crew was small, a group of four that didn't mind putting in that work if necessary. It was me, Keith, and the twins Jay aka Justin and Dee aka Dustin. They were identical, the only way that you could tell them apart was from their tattoos. Other than that people would always get the two mixed up. I could tell my buddies apart with my eyes closed. The twins were straight killers, it was in their bloodstream. Keith was a cool laidback type of cat that was smooth. Underneath his smile and charm he was also ruthless and vicious if you ever crossed him. Then it was me, the brains of the operation. I was always thinking of more ways to make more money. At times I try my best to stay sucker free out here, but it's always that time and moment when I have to get my hands dirty. When that time comes I turn into a cold hearted and atrocious human being. I hated a snake ass individual, crossing me will cost you your life. Finally Keith and Dee arrived joining in on the conversation. We usually met up once a week to go over the numbers. Right now the operation was running smoothly without a crease or a wrinkle.

"I spoke with Alejandro earlier today, he stated that our shipment shall be in tomorrow. Gabriela will be meeting with us at the airstrip in the afternoon. Jay and Dee I really need for the both of you to be on point. I will have some shooters close by in cut just in case something goes wrong." I said.

"Them Mexicans don't want to fuck around and lose their lives." Dee pulled out his Glock 40.

"I'm ready to put this shit on the streets and make it do what it do. Or last supplier was cool but from what I hear from my partners in New York this shit is going to move." Keith said.

I'm looking forward to pushing some new shit out here in these streets. Keith partners from New York put us on to this new connect that had some raw coke. Shit liked that was rare and I planned on taxing a few of my customers. They were ready and busying blowing up my line to buy bricks from me. I was anxious to see what it will do, if everything is successful I planned on purchasing me a home in Miami and in Scottsdale, buy a jet, and make a few investments. For the reminder of the day I set back and kicked it with my buddies. We ordered food while Jay called some hoes over to keep them company. They were fly and looked good but I wasn't trying to deal with thirsty hoes. They sat back and watched us shoot pool while I took all of their money. My phone rang and it was Tichina calling me, I ended the game to talk to my baby. Hearing her soft voice made me realize why I was digging her ass. The women that Jay had over were talking and laughing loudly. Tichina asked who was that in the background and begin to start questioning me. I told her the truth, but bounced out of there because it was getting late. Tichina now had my undivided attention, no interruptions. I made it to my $250,000 home in Olympia Fields. At times I would get lonely being here alone in my five bedroom, three bath two- story home. I never invited a woman over here before, pretty much just a few trustworthy people that I can count on one hand know where I live. Tichina shared with me that she was nervous about meeting my family tomorrow, I assured her that my family was laid back and that she didn't have anything to worry about. We spoke on the phone for about another hour before she started to get sleepy. When she yawned three times in the row that was my clue to end the call.

"Good night beautiful and get you some beauty rest. I'm looking forward to hanging out with you tomorrow." I said.

"Good night Tee." Tichina blew me a kiss before hanging up.

I said my prayers and went to sleep, making sure that my three pipes were close by just in case I had to use them.

Chapter 10

Tichina

I jumped up out of my sleep in a pool of sweat. Last night I had a nightmare that I had been kidnapped by a four masked men. They had my hands tied and my mouth covered with tape. They beat and raped me repeatedly because I wouldn't tell them anything about Tee. One of the men put a gun to my temple. I woke up before he pulled the trigger. My heart was racing, my phone starting going off causing me to jump. Nervously I looked around for my phone in my bed. It was Tee sending me a good morning text message. I smiled and replied back, happy to know that it was just a bad dream. I got up and took care of my hygiene before I called to check on Kamara. An hour later I heard my door bell ringing. I already knew that it was either Kamara or Emani popping up over here. I peeped out the peep hole and seen Kamara and Karli. I opened up the door and little bitty Karli walked inside carrying a doll and a McDonald's bag.

"Don't you walk past your Tee Tee without speaking and not give me a hug." I said to Karli, she had a frown on her face.

"Girl don't mind her, she has an attitude this morning because she thought that she was going to bring all of her toys with her." Kamara said.

Karli gave me a hug and walked off to seat at the dining room table. I turned on my 60 in flat screen so that she could watch cartoons. Kamara sat on my couch looking a lot better than yesterday. She was definitely in good spirits today despite what all just went down the day before.

"What's up girl? What brings you by here so early?" I asked sitting next to her.

"I just don't want to be in the house all alone. It feels kind of weird now without Lil Dave being there. Tichina you know that we have been together for years."

"Do you miss him? Please don't tell me that you regret everything. Kamara you can always come here, my door is always open. Maybe you should move once your lease is up."

"Hell no I don't miss him. I'm afraid to be there. I keep thinking that he is going to come back for me. Moving is the first thing to do on my list in the next two months. I've been talking to Keith and he said that he would help me."

"Well you don't have anything to worry about because you changed the locks. So you and Keith are getting a little serious I see. That's cool, Keith is a nice comeback for you. Today is the day that I will be meeting Tee family. I'm nervous as fuck."

I got up and walked in the back to my room. I needed to figure out what I was about to wear. Kamara made sure that Karli was comfortable before she joined me in my bedroom. I was inside my closet trying to figure out what to wear. It was between three maxi dresses, you could never go wrong with a maxi dress. I laid them out on my bed. Kamara walked inside.

"I liked the soft pink tie dye one. You could wear a soft pink shade on your lips. The other two are see thru, you don't want to show his family all of your goods." Kamara laughed.

"I was thinking of going with that one as well with some pink sandals. Girl yesterday I ran into one of his ex-side chick at the beauty shop. She was indirectly talking mad shit about him to me. You know that I had to check the bitch real quick. I went off on Tee ass too, you know that I don't tolerate no drama of any kind."

"Damn, who is the bitch? What did Tee say about everything?" Kamara asked.

"Some bitch named Tootie, as a matter of fact I wonder if Emani knows anything about her. Tee was mad about everything and told me not to worry about the bitch. It wasn't as if I was worried about her in the first place."

I continued to talk Kamara ears off. No lie I was happy that she did pop up over here. She helped take away my nervousness that I had. Kamara talked about Keith like a high school girl. My friend was feeling him and mentally was moving on. Keith was cool and although he was Tee friend he bet not hurt her. I just wanted my friend to be happy. The clock was ticking and two pm was approaching. I was prepared to meet up with Tee. Kamara helped me get prepared making sure that I was straight. She was going to stay at my place because she didn't feel comfortable at her own home. I left her my extra keys. Before pulling off I Facetime called Tee making sure that I had the correct address. He picked up and was outside grilling with Keith and twins standing next to him. Quickly I thought of an idea, Kamara should join me.

"Hey bighead I'm on my way. Hey fellas." I spoke to everyone. Keith asked for Kamara, I told him that she was in my house and staying because she didn't have a babysitter.

"Tell Kamara that she could bring her daughter. We love the kids." Tee said laughing and joking.

"Cool, let me call you back."

I hung up the phone and went back inside to see Kamara and Karli looking bored as hell. "Kamara, Tee said it was fine if you brought Karli. Keith asked for you as well, please come with me."

"Tichina I have to change my clothes. I can't wear this."

I looked at Kamara up and down. "I have a maxi dress to match your red sandals." Kamara changed into my dress, she was thicker than me and was rocking it. "I don't even want my dress back anymore Big Booty Judy. You look very nice, all you need is some Ruby Woo."

She put on some lipstick and was ready to roll, leaving her car parked in front of my house. One hour later we finally made it to Tinley Park. We pulled up in front of a gorgeous patio home that was surrounded by acres of grass. Damn, Tee grandma was living fabulous. We all sat in the car amazed at the lovely home. It wasn't like we haven't seen a beautiful home before, it's just that many black people don't live like his not unless they purchase a home like this down south. I called Tee and told him that I was parked out front. Before we stepped out of the car Kamara and I both checked our teeth, hair, and face out. We had to make sure that we was on point. Tee and Keith met up with us in the front. Karli was looking at the both of them strangely, she went into stranger danger mode. Tee and Keith was happy to see the both of us.

"Hello pretty what's your name? Keith asked Karli.

"Karli, what's your name and whose house is this?" Karli little grown ass asked.

We all started laughing as we followed Tee and Keith to the back yard. Tee held on to my hand making it known that I was his woman. When we made it to the back it was a backyard full of people. Everyone turned to look at us as if we were royal. I squeezed Tee's hand tightly as I became more nervous. Tee guided me toward his grandma, the sweet older lady was sitting at a big table surrounded by other family members. She was beautiful, Tee resembled her. Her hair was white and cut into a bob. Her skin was brown and had very few wrinkles. She smiled as if she was looking forward to meeting me. Maybe Tee had already told her about me.

"Grandma this is Tichina. Tichina this is my grandmother Pearl the woman who raised me."

"Hello nice to meet you." I said but she cut me off from talking.

"Hey girl come on over here and give me hug. She's very beautiful just like you described her Tavion. You can call me Pearl, just like everyone else. I heard so much about you Miss Tichina, please make yourself comfortable and welcome to my home." Grandma Pearl said.

I smiled, embracing her back. "Nice to meet you Pearl." She went on to introduce me to everyone who was sitting at the table. They all spoke back and complimented me. Grandma Pearl called Keith over to her table. "Keith bring your friend over here, you know better than that."

Keith, Kamara, and Karli walked over to the table. "Hello there, I'm grandma Pearl and who are you pretty?"

"Hi, I'm Karli," she smiled.

"Come over and give me a hug."

"This is my friend Kamara and Karli is her daughter. Kamara and Tichina are friends." Keith said.

"Hey Kamara, you're beautiful as well. Child you have a shape out of this world. Look at you with them curves. Keith you're going to have to keep the men away from this one." Grandma Pearl joked and said.

We all laughed. "Thank you and nice to meet you." Kamara said.

"Welcome to my home ladies, eat and enjoy yourself."

Okay that went pretty well, now I felt the nervousness going away. We took a seat at the table and the gentlemen went to go make our plates. Karli asked if she could go over to play with the children. Kamara give her permission and told her to have fun. The twins came over from playing basketball all sweaty. We spoke to them and they gave us a hug. Jay introduced us to his baby mother Shay, their daughter was over there playing with the other children. Shay seemed quiet and shy, totally opposite from the type of girl whom I would think to be with Jay. I mean I didn't really know the twins, but I did hear that they didn't play any games out here in these streets. Dee walked over with his baby mother. She wobbled over to our table as he carried several plates full of food. Kamara and I both looked at one another. I know that we was thinking the same thing, this must be Dee's baby mother. She was huge, very pretty, pregnancy had her skin so clear and bright.

"This is my woman and the soon to be mother of my child, Dasia. Dasia this is Tichina and Kamara." Dee introduced us.

"Hey Dasia, nice to meet you. How many months are you?"

"Girl I'm six months pregnant with twins." Dasia smiled, I know I'm huge."

"Congratulations, that's so awesome. I know that you're happy to be having twins." Me and Kamara said.

"Yes and I'm not having any more after this." Dasia laughed.

So far Shay and Dasia seemed cool, I didn't pick up a bad vibe from them. Tee and Keith walked back over to the table with our food and we started to eat. He asked me if I was cool and said that he was going to talk to the fellas. I was straight, hell I was happy that Kamara was with me. The men walked off, leaving us ladies alone at the table. We all began to talk with one another as if we knew each other for a very long time. Shay and Dasia gave a brief description of their lives, where they was from, their ages, what they did for a living. Shay was twenty seven and was a Physical Therapist at Illinois Masonic Medical Center. Dasia was twenty five and a Chef who owned her own catering business called Dasia's Dining. I see that the ladies was on their shit and doing big things. In the future if they're not messy and like to keep bullshit up, maybe we can grow and be friends. Time from time the fellas would come and check on us to see how we were doing. After hours had gone by and the sun was going down Tee asked me to join him privately in the house. Kamara said that Karli was ready to go, so Keith offered to take them home. I gave Kamara and Karli a hug and told her to call me as soon as she made it to her car. They left, Tee and I went into his grandmother's home. The cool air hit me as soon as I walked inside. The inside was lovely just like I imagined that it would be. I looked around and stared at the family portraits that were hanging on the wall. I laughed at a picture of Tee, he was snaggletooth and still looked the same. I noticed a picture of a pregnant woman and man together. She resembled grandma Pearl. I wondered if that was Tee's mother and father. If so, Tee looked exactly liked his mom, he noticed that I was staring at the picture.

He stood behind me and wrapped his arms around my waist. "That's my mother and father. My mother name was

Shelia and my father name was Troy. My mother died shortly after giving birth to me. During child birth the doctors gave my mother an incorrect dosage of medication which made her lungs and heart collapse. My father was a heavy smoker and died of lung cancer five years ago."

"Oh my God, I'm so sorry that you had to grow up not knowing your mother and to turn around and lose your father. Did your family sue the hospital?"

"Yes they sued Cook County Hospital, they settled and I was given two hundred thousand at the age of twenty one. That's when I moved my granny from Englewood to here and bought her this house. It was the least that I could do since she raised me. Did you enjoy yourself and the food today?"

"I really enjoyed myself, your grandmother and family is really cool. The food was delicious, I'm so full that I could fall out."

Tee laughed. "Do you have to go straight home? Do you mind hanging out at my place?"

I stared back at Tee looking at him as if he was serious. All I was thinking at he moment is, this nigga just want some pussy. Tee picked up on my facial expression immediately.

"Look I'm not on anything. I swear I'll be under my best behavior." He smiled.

Due to my past I had a problem with trusting men. So far Tee made me feel as though I could trust him. If he just wanted to fuck me, he wouldn't have introduced me to his family and friends.

"Sure I will go to your place, where do you live?" I asked.

"In Olympia Fields, just follow me precious."

Tee and I went back outside to where everyone was at. I said good bye to everyone and grandma Pearl gave me a big hug. "Don't be a stranger now, you hear me? As a matter of fact store my number in your phone and call me whenever you'll like to talk." Grandma Pearl gave me her phone number, I stored it in my phone as Tee watched from afar. He smiled, apparently he was happy that his grandma and I was creating a bond. I stored Shay and Dasia numbers as well, they seemed like go getters and women that was on something. I was too old to be partying, hanging out in clubs, and to be fighting outside. Maybe becoming familiar with some new women would smart, don't get it twisted Kamara and Emani will always be my best friends. I went ahead and waited in my car for Tee. As I was waiting I received a call from Emani.

"What's up Emani?" I answered my phone, I haven't heard from Emani all day.

"What are you Tichina? Girl tonight it's a party that I want you to attend with me. Are you down?" Emani was pumped up.

"Girl I'm just now leaving Tee's grandma house. Unfortunate I will have to decline your invite to the party tonight. Tee and I are about to call it a night and head in, I'm spending the night at his place."

"Awe snap! Please don't tell me that you're about to get shit popping tonight. Tichina you and Tee are really getting serious, I see." Emani laughed

"He's cool and no I didn't say that I was going to fuck him. Girl, I'll call you back tomorrow, he just pulled on the side. Goodbye crazy."

Tee was sitting on the side of me in his car. He told me to follow him back to his place. It take us too long to arrive at his place. His house was nice just like I expected. I asked for a drink so that I could relax and ease off some of the skittish feeling that I had. Tee poured me some red wine and we begin to get better acquitted, just the two of us.

Chapter 11

Emani

Bummer I didn't have anyone to go out with me tonight. I called Kamara, she was with Keith and then Tichina was chilling with Tee. From the outside looking in I can see that my two best friends were starting to fall in love with these niggas. Honestly I feel as though that they're both moving too fast. Especially Kamara, just the other day we were fighting another bitch of her baby daddy. I can understand why Tichina can think that Tee is the man for her, because she has had her share of fucked up situations with men. It's was very rare for her to meet a gentlemen such as Tee. From my little personal background check that I did on Tee and his crew, I found out that they were paid and respected. If Tichina plays her cards right, then she could definitely win the spot of his number one girl. There was no way that Tee wasn't fucking another woman, he had too much money. I just hope that Tichina doesn't give him the pussy for free tonight, if she fucks him she better have something to show for it. I know that she got a bracelet, dinners, and a few gifts out of him, but that's small things compared to what Tee really has to offer. I was upset that my friends was with their men and that I was fighting with mine. Ty and I haven't had sex since he beat me with a belt. He hasn't been coming home at night and when he does come home and gets in bed with me, he doesn't touch me. Earlier today while he was in the shower I took his car keys and went through his car. Ty has been acting suspicious to me, always having his phones glued to his body. Whenever he received a phone call, he would walk away from some privacy. As long as I've been with Ty he's never kept anything from me, well that's what I thought until I found out about the secret insurance policy that he had on me. I went through his car as quick as I could, inside the glove compartment, in between the seat, etc. When I searched the back seat of his car, I found a cheap, colorful, pineapple shaped earring. I took the earing and placed it inside my pocket and went back inside the house. Ty was still in the bathroom, so I put his keys back. I was mad at the fact that I found an earring in the car. The type of earring made me feel as though it belonged to a young girl. Thoughts start going through my head of Ty messing around with a younger girl. He stepped out of the bathroom talking on the phone, not paying me any attention at all. As mad as I was I didn't speak upon finding a pineapple earring in his car, out of fear that he would beat my ass again. Instead I spent some quality time with my children by taking them to the waterpark. I needed to get out of the house quick, fast and in a hurry before I went off. When I returned home Ty was no longer there and had left a big mess in the bedroom. I called to check his ass, but he didn't answer. Instead he hit me back with a text message saying that he was busy and that he would call me later. The children beg me to go over their grandmother house. I called Big Momma and she said that it was fine for them to spend a week with her. I made sure that I packed enough clothing for my three children and dropped them off at their granny house. Big Momma was happy to see me and my children. She was busy cooking a big meal for the family. I stayed over to help her out and to make sure that she wasn't disobeying her diabetic diet. Big Momma has Type 2 diabetes, she was diagnosed five years ago. All of the family members made sure that she was taking her insulin and controlling her blood sugar. We've had quite a few scares which led Big Momma to be admitted in the hospital. A few of my cousins were over at Big Mommas house too. We all ate, spending time with Big Momma was very important to me because tomorrow isn't always promised. It was getting late so I prepared to leave. Before leaving I gave Lil Ty, Tyshawn, and Tyesha a hug. I made them all promised that they would be under their best behavior. Tyshawn told me, "I love you momma" in sign language. I was so happy that he was getting better with signing, I told him that I love him so much. Although I had three children, Tyshawn was my favorite and needed the most attention because of his disability. I went home to an empty house, bored out of my mind. I wanted to go out and party, I could use a drink.

Club Ontourage was packed and jumping tonight as I pushed through the crowd. I decided to go out tonight by myself, instead of sitting in the house bored. Hell I didn't have my children so why not go out and enjoy myself. I spoke to a few people that I knew from the streets. I wasn't the type to mingle with just anyone so I stood back and watched the party. Occasionally I would dance to the music as the dee jay did his thang. It was some stunners in the house tonight. I laughed as I sipped on my patron watching them blow their money. My eyes scan the room as I searched for a potential side nigga that I could add to my life. My eyes had to be deceiving me when I saw Ty, Bari and some dark skinned chick talking. Ty had his arm wrapped around her tiny waist. She was attractive and had a voluptuous ass to back it up. Ty giggled in her ear and they both took a seat down on the couch. The woman sat in between Ty and Bari, from what it looked like Bari might've known her. Their facial expressions and body language gave it was, but I wasn't for sure yet. I gulped down my drink and ordered another one, a young man tried to flirt with me but I brushed him off. I had to focus on Ty to see what he was up to. He and the woman got closer as he whispered in her ear. My heart dropped and begin to burn inside. Bari got up to leave out of the club. I looked at my Rolex to check the time, we had at least one more hour to party. I pulled my phone out to text Ty, just to see how he would respond.

Me: Hey luv, when r u coming home?

Ty looked down at his phone and read the text message. He replied back to me.

Ty: Handling business right now. Not sure what time.

I didn't even bothered to text him back. He was handling business alright with his hand on her thigh. I wanted to go over there and fuck him up. The bartender asked if I wanted another drink before the bar closed. I declined, I had to be on point for what I planned on doing. I left the club and made it to my car. I parked three cars down from Ty's car and waited for him to exit the club. Ten minutes later Ty and the woman exited the club and strolled over to his car. She was intoxicated as she giggled over to the car with Ty's hand on her ass. Ty got behind the wheel and pulled off trying to maintain my distance. He remained on the streets, turning left on Ohio heading toward Michigan Ave, going the opposite way to the hotel. Five minutes later he pulled up in front of the Omni Chicago Hotel. He pulled into the self-parking garage, I was two cars behind him. As I searched for a parking spot my eyes began to get watery. Ty and the big booty hoe strolled inside the hotel to get a room. Enough of the games and the bullshit, I banged on the room door of 515. Ty and his whore remained quiet behind the other side of the door. My finger was covering the peephole. I knocked on the door again, Ty swung the door open with a pistol in his hand.

"Hey bae, what are you doing here?" Ty was shirtless and drunk, the Patron smell smacked me in the face.

"What's up with you and her?" I stepped inside the room. She was lying across the bed in her bra and thong.

"Babe, she's one of the new women. I was just chilling and explaining everything to her." Ty rubbed the side of my face. "You're more than welcome to join us."

I smacked Ty's hand away. "Join you, don't fucking play with Ty!"

Ty pulled me over to the corner and whispered in my ear. "Bae please don't act crazy, you know a threesome is all I ever wanted. We've been fighting like crazy, for once let's have some fun."

I looked over at the woman, she was very attractive. I've never been with a girl before, but Ty has asked me to have a threesome a number of times. Lately we have been fighting and I was tired of it. If having a threesome was going to put the happiness back into our home then I was going to it.

"Okay Ty I will have a threesome, but only one time and this is between the three of us." I said.

"I promise this will be our secret." Ty kissed me and led me to the bed. "This is my woman, Emani who I told you about. Emani this is Tootie, she's going to replace Sunshine."

"Hello Emani, nice to meet you. Ty has told me a lot of nice things about you." Tootie smiled as she licked her lips.

"Did I do really great with picking her?" Ty helped Tootie stand up so that I could view her body. Tootie took a spin with the help of Ty. Her body was banging and demanded attention.

"Yes you did a wonderful job babe." I said.

"Great, let's get this party started." Ty kissed me as Tootie watched and sipped on her drink. I took the cup out of her hand and gulped it down. It was Patron, I needed another shot if I was going to please Ty. I grabbed the bottle of Patron and drank as much as I could.

I rolled over to lie on Ty's chest. I looked around the bed and seen that Tootie wasn't here. As a matter of fact she was gone and so was her things. I sat up, my heading starting spinning as I rethought of all things that I did last night. I grabbed my head and rubbed my temples. I can't believe that I had licked and sucked on another woman's pussy. The thought of it made my stomach hurt. I ran to the bathroom and started throwing up. I can still smell her scent on me, I flushed the toilet. Quickly I got into the shower and allowed the hot water to wash away her scent. As the moments from last night replayed in my head I started to cry. I scrubbed my skin very hard, I felt dirty and used. I took my time taking my shower and rinsed my mouth out over and over. When I stepped out Ty was talking on the phone. I put on my things preparing to leave, Ty put up his finger indicating for me to give him a second. At this moment I didn't want to talk to him or hear what he had to say. Ty got off the phone and looked over at me.

"Please don't start with the craziness Emani, everything was all good last night. We're finally back down and I plan on putting Tootie to work ASAP. Thank you for having fun with me last night. I will always love you for that." Ty tried to give me a hug, but I knocked his hands away.

"Ty don't you ever think that it's going to happen again. If I find out that you and that bitch is fucking I'm done with you. I promise Ty, I will cut you off and you will never see me or the children again. I don't know how I allowed you to talk me into having a threesome in the first place."

"You know that you enjoyed it when she was eating your pussy or else you would've not came three times. Emani you don't have to worry about me fucking her again. It's only business being handled from here on out."

"Ty I wish that I could believe you, but I can't. I will see you when you get home."

I got up to leave out of the hotel and never looked back. I was blessed that walls couldn't talk to reveal the moments that went down.

Chapter 12

Tichina

Tee held me as I laid in his arms while he was asleep. I couldn't believe that I actually had sex with him last night. The innocent, sweet woman in me tried her best not to give him them pussy last night. I couldn't hold back any longer when Tee and I took a shower together. He had muscles that would make any woman want to hop on his dick. Speaking of which, that's exactly what I did. I looked down to see that Tee was hard and ready for more.

I grabbed his hard dick, Tee mumbled "You trying to rape me again?" He started laughing but I wasn't. I rolled over away from Tee and began to cry. "What, did I do something wrong?" he rubbed my back.

I began to cry and balled up, not wanting Tee to touch me. The word rape made me think about that dark moment. Every now and then I would go back to that bad place. "You didn't do anything wrong. Please try not to use the word rape around me."

"Damn, I'm so sorry babe. I totally forgot all about that."
Tee turned me around to face him. "Sweetheart I will never
ever hurt you or allow anyone else to. I promise to always
protect to you."

"I'm sorry that I started crying, you must think that I'm
crazy." I wiped away my tears, all I wanted to do right now
was make love to Tee. I pushed him down onto the bed and
straddled on top of him. I didn't care about him not wearing
a condom. I trusted him, I needed him, I fucked him like I
was Jada Fire. Tee thrusted deep inside of me making feel
all eleven inches. He filled me up unlike no other man. I
started shaking, my eyes rolled to the back of my head.

"Oh yes! Oh yes!" I came so hard on his dick. I didn't want
to get off of him, the feeling was refreshing.

"Damn Tichina, you hiding something from me? I feel like
you took all your anger out on my dick." Tee laughed.

"You have no idea how long that I've been wanting you
inside of me. Tee please don't judge me or look at me any
different."

"Look at you different? You're a grown ass woman, my
woman. For the record that pussy is now mine, all you is

mine. Let's get dress and do some shopping on Michigan Ave."

We both showered together and we couldn't keep our hands off each either. We got dressed and rode in Tee's Maserati. He allowed me to drive him around today while he sat in the passenger seat. We made it downtown in forty minutes and self-parked on Michigan and Ohio. We walked The Magnificent Mile shopping at Bloomingdales, Saks Fifth Avenue and Nordstrom's. Tee said that I could have whatever I liked. He pulled out his black card, charging everything that I wanted. Shopping was something that I truly enjoyed to do. I bought swimsuits, shades, shoes, clothes, etc. Tee purchased one thing and that was a pair of Versace shades. We walked hand in hand, from store to store. A girl could get used to this on a daily basics. My stomach staring talking, that's when I realized that I didn't have nothing to eat except for a donut. Tee was hungry as well so we both decided to have a seat at Grand Lux Café. It was pretty busy in here, thank goodness we didn't have to wait too long to be seated. We were seated at a booth in the corner of the restaurant. I was ready to place my order not wasting anytime when the waiter came to our table.

Meanwhile

Ain't this some bullshit that I'm viewing right about now?! Tee and that bitch from the beauty shop was sitting across from me and my friend Bridget while we enjoyed our lunch. Bridget was busy running her mouth about something that wasn't as important as this.

"Shhhh." I put up my right hand as if I was directing a choir and told her to mute it.

Bridget stopped running her mouth as she took a look over her shoulder. She witnessed the same thing that I did, turned around and waited for me to respond. I was salty as fuck that Tee was with that chick for real. When I first seen her in the beauty shop I thought that maybe she would be just one of his fun girls, nothing serious. Seeing that they have been doing some major shopping today displayed that ole girl was possibly his new chick. I felt so embarrassed in front of Bridget but tried to act as if the shit didn't faze me at all. Our waiter walked past and I order another Mai Tai. Since I've last seen Tee he hasn't been checking for me period. I must admit that after our last visit I knew that he was going to cut me off. Usually Tee would pull a stunt like this but still manage to come back to me.

"Damn Tootie looks like ole girl has a hold on your boo."
Bridget hating ass laughed and said.

"Fuck you Bridget, besides it's only a matter of time when
he would be running back. You Tee and I have a history."

"Girl you aren't going to be nothing but just a fun girl to
Tee. No wife or nothing special, just a fuck buddy. You
know that I'm the friend that's going to keep it real with
you."

I rolled my eyes, the waiter handed me my Mai Tai. I was
boiling inside and filled with jealousy and hate. I was
starting to feel my drink, it was my third Mai Tai. "I should
go over there and smack the shit out of him and her ass." I
took a move to get up, but Bridget pushed me back down.

"No in the hell you won't embarrass me in this restaurant.
You know damn well that Tee would fuck you up and then
I would have to get in it. I just got my hair done and this
lace frontal wasn't cheap." Bridget flipped her hair.

"Let's hurry up and leave, the sight of them too is making
me sick to my stomach. If I sit here much longer I don't
think that I could control my anger."

Bridget paid the bill and grabbed my hand like I was her
child ushering me down the escalator. I tried to break out of

her grip and march over to where Tee and that bitch was sitting. Before approaching the escalator Tee and I made eye contact with one another. Outside Bridget and I waited for the valet to bring our cars around. The driver pulled my Audi truck in front and I hopped in and pulled off quickly burning rubber. I pulled out my cell phone to call Ty.

"Hey Ty what's up, I need to meet up with you to discuss what we were talking about last night. Meet me at my place, 1 East Delaware Place right off State Street."

"Cool I'll meet you there in an hour." Ty said.

"Great, I'll be waiting for you."

Ty hit my line and told me that he was downstairs. I buzzed him and made sure that I looked good in my tank top and leggings. I spritz some Flower Bomb behind my ears, on my neck, and between my legs. I was low key crushing on Ty and enjoyed the threesome that we had other night with his woman. Emani was weak and easy to manipulate, getting rid of her would be easy. Ty tapped on my door and I opened for him to enter. I gave him a big hug and he grabbed my ass as he hugged me back. Ty looked and smelled good that I had to fuck him again before he left my place.

"Make yourself comfortable, would you like something to drink?" I offered.

"Yeah, do you have some Patron?" Ty asked.

"Yes I do, coming up." I walked over to my bar to pour us both a glass of Patron and dropped two ice cubes in the glasses.

When I walked to take a seat next to him on the couch I made sure that my ass jingled. Ty eyes watched my ass and licked his lips.

"So I want to touch on what we discussed last night at the club. Like I told you before I'm down with setting up niggas, but before you send me off on anyone I think that I have a person in mind."

"Who is the person that you're talking about?" Ty seemed curious as he sipped on his drink.

"His name is Tee from Englewood, him and his crew run a very profitable operation. That have a great connect with it comes to cocaine. I heard, well I know for sure that pretty soon won't anyone be able to get their hands on the best coke without going through him first."

"I think I heard of this nigga Tee before. I heard you mentioned crew, who is his crew?"

"There is Keith, he's the smart one. Then the twins, Dee and Jay, they are the killers. Tee is the go getter, a business man, never slacking when it comes to making money."

"How do you know so much about these niggas? Which one did you use to fuck?" Ty asked.

Ty was very smart I see, he picked up fast. "I used to fuck with Tee for many years. When they started off they used to get down at my house. From there they've grown overtime and made at least a million or more a piece. They are very selective of who they allow around them. They always keep a low profile and their very respected. Please keep this between you and me if you plan on taking him out. They are untouchable and not easy to get close to."

"No one is untouchable. Do you have pictures of these niggas?"

"Yes I do." I pulled out my IPad, went to my photos, and shared the few photos that I did have on them. They're photos from events and parties that I attended with them. Looking at Tee's pictures made me feel bad about setting him up. That quickly went away when I had a quick flashback of him and that bitch in the restaurant. Ty looked at the different pictures, he gave me back my IPad.

"Let's get started on him tomorrow. Do you still deal with him? How close are you two? What information do you have on him that can be helpful?" Ty asked finishing off his drink.

"I know where his grandmother lives. I don't know exactly where Tee lives, but that shouldn't be hard to find out. He has three successful businesses and several properties. He also has three vehicles a Jaguar, Porsche Truck, and at the moment he's driving his Aston Martin. Keith drives a Lamborghini and the Twins, Jay and Dee both drive Maybach's one white and the other black."

"Cool I will run this through Bari and if everything that you're telling me is true, then we're on his ass. Right now be a real woman and come straighten me out." Ty looked at me slyly with lust in his eyes.

I knew what he wanted and I wanted it as bad as him. Ty handsome, chocolate ass didn't have to ask me to take care of him because that was on my do to list. I unzipped his pants and pulled out his rock hard dick and begin to suck and spit all over it. I knew that Ty was testing my sexual skills to see if I could manipulate these niggas out of their money. I already passed the threesome test, now was the time to show him my one on one skills. I gagged giving him messy, sloppy, noisy head. I gave him eye attention and watched as he tried his best to hold back that nut. I sucked and slurped it up, it shot out of him like a sprinkler. My pretty, brown face was covered with his sperm.

"You have enlisted a female beast babe. I will have those niggas falling in love and opening up. By the time that they realized what hit them I'll be long gone."

"Let's get this money baby." Ty said grinning.

Back To Tichina

After our long day of shopping Tee and I made it back to his place by six pm. While we were shopping Tee convinced me to stay the night with him again. I didn't have a problem with that being that I had purchased new apparel, underwear included. I explained to him that I parked so far and then jumped on the bus to get to work. Tee didn't like that and told me that he would pay for my monthly parking so that I could park in the lot closes to my job. Hearing that made me happy so I agreed to stay another night. Things seemed to be moving fast, but it felt so right and real. It was like Tee and I have been together forever. While Tee was in the bathroom I went stooping through some of his things. I ran across a picture of him and brown skinned girl. On the back of the picture it said, 'My One True Love.' This had to be the girl Shay who Tee spoke upon. They both appeared young and very much in love on this picture. I continued to go through the rest of his drawer and found many more photos of the two of them. Damn, I couldn't believe that Tee could just stop loving someone so easily after so many years. Suddenly I felt self-conscious and doubted if Tee would ever really love me that way. Or if I was just filling in the empty spot until Shay was released. I dropped the photos onto the floor when I heard Tee behind me. It was too late to hide what I was doing, I had been busted.

"Curiosity killed the cat." Tee said

"I'm so sorry Tee, please forgive me for going through your things." He walked over and helped me pick up the pictures. "Do I have to worry about her Tee? She's your first true love, should I be threaten?"

"Threaten about what? I already told you that what Shay and I had is over with. Do I still love her? Yes I do, but I'm not in love with her. You have nothing to worry about and over time I will prove that to you. That's if you allow me to do that."

"Tee I care about you, it's been a while since I've cared about a man. You're different, sincere, and mature. Just please don't hurt me, please I can't bear the pain." I cried softly.

Tee wiped away the tears, "You have to let go of that pain or else it will eat you up inside. We both have a past that, but we have to leave the past in the past. The pain has to be removed in order for love to come inside."

Tee kissed me on my forehead, we both stood there in silence. Everything that he was saying was the truth. I wasn't going to allow my past to interfere with my present. Black men such as Tee are extinct in the 2000's. I had him right now, we were both single with no children. No extra baggage, it was time for me to drop my bags and retire from being that bag lady who Erkyah Badu was singing about. Right now I was finally going to surrender myself to Tee.

"I have big plans for the both us Tichina. I like you and apparently so does my grandmother. You have your head on straight, not into partying, you're not messy, and don't have a name for yourself. First I have to make sure if you could cook or not before I know if you're wife material." Tee laughed.

"I can cook my ass off Mr. I learned from the best, my mother is a beast in the kitchen. Maybe next weekend you can meet my parents. In the meantime I will have to show off my cooking skills for you."

"I would like that, right now I have a taste for something else." Tee played with my clit indicating that he wanted a taste of my tropical starburst flavored pussy. We went to lay down and made love in his California king size bed. From this point on it was me and Tee against the world and no bitch from the past named Shay or Tootie was going to come between the two of us.

Chapter 13

Kamara

Keith and I have been have been enjoying one another more than a lot lately. I was digging Keith street ass, he was different from Lil Dave lame ass. Speaking of Lil Dave that bastard hasn't called to check on his daughter since the fight. His bust down girlfriend called up to my job and tried to get my fired once she discovered that her funds had been stolen. My boss didn't believe her and by that time I had covered my tracks at work, claiming that she was stalking me. Emani gave me seventy percent of her money, keeping thirty percent. I put the money away and planned on using it just in case I ran into a rainy day. With the help of Keith I was moving into my three bedroom home in Elmhurst. This was something that I always planned on doing but Lil Dave was on some little boy games. After so many years of working at Chase I knew everything that was to know about grants, loans, and the importance of having good credit. With a credit score of 810 it wasn't a bank that wouldn't give me a loan with a low interest rate. I will be moving into my new home two weeks from now. When I told Karli about the good news she was so excited. She through me off guard when she asked me if her daddy was going to live with us. It was very hard for me to tell her that her father and I would never be together again. Karli started to cry which made me cry as well. This is why I fought hard to keep my family together because I knew how much she loved her trifling father. Karli was starting to see more of Keith around, so I wasn't surprised when she asked me if Keith was her new daddy. I had to explain to her that Keith and I was dating but he wasn't going to move in with us. I made sure that she was fine with Keith being around. The last thing that I wanted to do was date someone that made my daughter feel uncomfortable. At the end of it all Karli was very important to me and her opinion matter the most. Karli and I talked as we sipped tea and ate lemon cake at her small table. After our talk she was happy about getting a bigger room and going to a new school. I made it very clear that it was going to be just the two of us.

Today was my day off and I was spending it with Keith furniture shopping for my new home. Yes I had put it on him so that he could break that bread off the right way, on me. Never in my life have a man spoiled me before. With

Keith it was different, I liked him it wasn't just about the money. With Keith I felt protected, something that I've never felt with Lil Dave before. Coming from my background I've never had anyone to protect me. Inside the furniture store Keith spent ten stacks on me. I was very excited about moving into my home that I planned on moving in once my furniture arrived. Once we were done we picked up Karli from summer camp and also grabbed a pizza and some wings. We were riding in Keith's new Cadillac truck down Madison Street. Out of all the buses to pull on the side of us why did it have to be the bus that Lil Dave was driving? He looked down inside the car and noticed that it was me and his daughter in the truck with another man. I locked eyes with him, Li Dave eyes filled with rage as he looked at Karli in the back seat. The light turned green, Keith pulled off continuing to drive down Madison. I told him that Lil Dave was on the side of us driving the CTA bus and had seen us. Lil Dave stopped letting passengers on and off the bus, but still managed to catch up with us in traffic. On the intersection of Madison and Kostner what happened next shocked the hell out of me. Lil Dave came full speed driving toward us trying to hit Keith's truck.

"What the fuck is dude on?!" Keith drove faster barely hitting several cars and pedestrians.

Lil Dave kept on coming for us hitting several cars driving erratically. He wasn't going stop until he caught up with us. "Turn off down a side street so that we could lose him!" Lil Dave was running lights with passengers on the bus. Keith whipped a sharped left on Kilpatrick with Lil Dave barely missing us. Karli was screaming and crying hysterically. "It's okay baby, everything will be okay." Keith pulled over to make sure that we were straight. Lil Dave left his bus unattended and ran across the street.

"Bitch you got my daughter around another nigga!" He tried to pull open the car door. Keith ran around the car and stuck him. They both started fighting, Karli was crying and calling out for her father. Keith knocked Lil Dave out cold and pulled out his gun aiming it at him. "I should finish your ass here, right now for disrespected me." Keith was angry. No one ever fucked with him and live to see the other day no matter what the situation was.

"Daddy! Daddy!" Karli screamed from the back seat of the truck.

"Noooo Keith, please not in front of my daughter." I got out of the car, stood on the side of Keith begging and pleading for him to put the gun down.

"What you going to shoot me in front of my daughter, in front of everyone?!" Lil Dave held his jaw, his face displayed a sinister grin.

"You asking to die nigga, but I'm going to spare you in front of your daughter!"

I pulled onto Keith's arm, we both got back inside his truck. Karli and both and I were crying while Keith held a straight face. Lil Dave ran back across the street and got back on the bus pulling off. Karli was shaking so I held her as we went home. "It's alright baby, mommy is here and everything is okay."

Three hours later I was finally able to get Karli to sleep. My nerves were still jumping so I popped a Xanax. An hour ago I called Tichina and Emani to tell them about the crazy shit that went down. They seemed worried about my safety and suggested that I get the police involved. I disagreed, how was I going to be able to go to the police? Then they apprehend Lil Dave and he tells them about

Keith. Keith was very upset and still wanted to kill him, telling me that next time Lil Dave won't be so lucky. The Xanax was starting to get kick in causing me to get drowsy. I drifted off to sleep and started dreaming about the events from earlier. My dream ended differently this time with Keith shooting Lil Dave down in front of me and his daughter. Lil Dave laid covered with bullet holes on the ground. What was crazy was that Lil Dave didn't die no matter how many times that Keith shot him. Lil Dave turned red with flames surrounding his body. I started running and crying making sure that he wouldn't get to or Karli. I hid Karli in an abandoned building, I don't know what happened to Keith he was no longer there. Lil Dave caught up with me and punched me in the face. I felt the pain of the punches as if they were real. **Pow**! **Pow**! I jumped out of my dream to Lil Dave on top of me. At first I thought that I was hallucinating off the Xanax and shit but I wasn't. Lil Dave was on top of me beating my ass.

"Surprise to see me bitch?! Where is your boyfriend at now?! He's not here to save your ass!" **Pow**! **Pow**! **Pow**! Lil Dave continued to punch me in my head.

"How did you get in here? Help! Help! Help!" I cried and screamed.

"Shut the fuck up hoe before you wake up Karli." **Pow!**
Pow! Pow!

I bit Lil Dave on the arm. "Ouch, you silly bitch!" **Pow!**
The last punch knocked me out for minutes. Some liquid
splashed in my face snapping me back into reality.
Whatever it was Lil Dave was pouring it all over my body
from an Aquafina water bottle while I laid in bed. When I
smelled it I realized that it was gasoline. I got up with the
little strength that I had but Lil Dave punched me again.

"Karli help! Karli help!" I screamed praying that she would
hear me. "Help! Help!" I was moving in slow motion, dizzy
from the fumes that were fucking with my breathing. God
answered my prayers, Karli came running into the room.

"Daddy what are you doing to mommy? Please don't hurt
her, I love mommy!" Karli stood by the door watching her
father harm me.

"Karli baby go call 911, go get help baby!"

"Karli go back in your room sweetie while your mother and
I finish talking." Lil Dave said as he held the lighter in his
hand.

"Karli please listen to mommy and go get help now!"

Karli ran off, Lil Dave tried to run behind her, but my baby girl was fast. I managed to pick up the hammer from the side of my bed. Lil Dave threw me across the bed and jumped back on top of me. I hit him in the head with the hammer, blood started gushing out of his head.

"Just for that you're about to burn hoe!" Keith sparked the lighter, the bed and I was on fire. I cried as I tried to put the fire out. My skin was burning, the pain was excruciating. Lil Dave set his goofy ass on fire too. He grabbed on to me causing both of us to burn together.

"Help! Help! Help! I fell out of the bed kicking Lil Dave off me. "Help! Cough, cough, Help!" I screamed until I passed off from the smoke.

Karli went to knock on the neighbor door to get help. My next door neighbor came and discovered me and Lil Dave burning. She called 911 and immediately tried to put out the flames with fire extinguisher that were in the hallway on the wall. She dragged me out of the room and performed CPR on me until help arrived.

I laid in the hospital bed unconscious but I could still hear the voices surrounding me. There was a lot of praying and crying over me. Tichina and Emani cried the hardest. I wanted to tell them to stop crying and that I was going to okay. The doctor came inside the room to discuss my condition.

"Hello everyone I'm Dr. Scott, the surgeon that operated on Kamara. She suffered severe burning in her lower extremities and a few places on her face. Please don't worry it's nothing that plastic surgery can't fix. The smoke damaged her lungs the endotracheal tube that's going through her mouth and is helping her breathe, air is being sucked to and from her lungs for respiration. She's definitely a fighter. If you have any more questions and concerns please don't mind to have Kamara's nurse to call or page me." Dr. Scott left out of the room.

After that I heard several people talking again. The doctor was right when he said that I was fighter. Everyone was worried about me, throughout the time I heard the one voice that I was waiting to hear.

"Mommy!" Karli grabbed my hand.

"Can I kiss mommy Auntie Tichina? Will it hurt if I kiss her?" Karli asked.

"Yes baby you can kiss her, it won't hurt at all." Tichina picked her up to give me a kiss.

Karli kissed me several times over and over again. Thank you God for protecting my baby girl. A tear trickled down my cheek. Karli became alarmed when she seen it. "Did I hurt mommy, why is she crying?" an innocent Karli cried.

"No you didn't hurt mommy. She's just happy that you are here." Tichina said.

Thanks Tichina, please tell my baby that she can kiss me as much as she likes. Tichina and Karli stayed with me when everyone left keeping me company. Karli began to get restless and laid next to me as Tichina spoke to me liked nothing changed. Moments later Keith walked inside, I could smell the Clive Christian No 1. He said hello to Tichina and Karli, they both were happy to see him and stepped out to give him some privacy. Keith touched my motionless body making me feel warm inside. He spoke with a crackled voice.

"I'm very sorry for taking a week to come up here to see you. When I first found out what happened I was so angry. All I could think about was the chance I had to kill that hoe ass nigga wishing that I did. I spoke with your doctor, he said that you're improving day by day. Kamara it's hard to see you going through this. I'm willing to do whatever it takes to get you back out of that bed. Karli need you, your friends need you, and so do I. I'm praying for you, I love you baby and when you pull through this I got you forever. I promise won't anyone ever hurt you again." Keith held my hand as he stroked my hair. He prayed over my body, who would've thought a gangsta like him could pray.

Overtime during my hospitalization I was improving with the help of bronchodilators, steroids, and antibiotics. The biggest thing that helped me pull through all of this was the love and support that I was receiving from my family and friends. My coworkers came by to show their support. My visitors didn't realize that I could hear them. One day when Tichina and Emani were visiting me they spoke about Tee. Emani was asking Tichina certain questions but Tichina dismissed her ass and told her to stop being nosy. When Tichina stepped out to use the washroom I could hear Emani make a phone call to someone. She told the caller that she didn't get the information and didn't feel comfortable betraying her friend. I couldn't believe what I just heard, Emani was foul as fuck right now. I wish that I could get up and smack the shit out of her ass. Tichina walked back into the room and Emani got off the phone. I moved around in bed trying to get Tichina's attention. Tichina rushed over to the bed while Emani went to get the doctors. The doctors and nurses rushed inside and told Tichina and Emani to leave the room. My eyes popped opened, all I seen was a bright white light. I became nervous and began to move around and start pulling on things. The medical staff held me down so that I didn't fall onto the floor. Seconds later I started to see them clearly, it was two Caucasian males, an African American and an Asian. They started placing things on my head and chest. "Relax Kamara you're in the hospital, I'm Dr. Scott." I started to relax and looked around the room as they did whatever they were doing. They talked among themselves speaking in medical jargon that I didn't understand. "You're doing fine Kamara, please don't pull out your ventilator it is helping you breathe." I cooperated because I heard the Asian woman asked if they should place me in restraints and I didn't want to be tied down. They were in my room performing test on me for a very long time. I was becoming restless and drifted off to sleep. I tried my best to stay up so that I could see everyone but whatever they gave me calmed my nerves and made me groggy.

Chapter 14

Tichina

Kamara scared the hell out of me when she jumped up yesterday at the hospital. All I could remember was that she was trying to get up out of the bed. The doctors ushered us out of the room too fast for me to say anything. They spent hours inside the room with her, but I waited patiently until they were done. Emani received a phone call from Ty and jumped up to leave like she usually does. By the time when the doctors stepped out it was close to 8pm. I spoke with Dr. Scott asking him how was Kamara condition. He said that she was doing fine and that if she keeps on improving that he would wean her off the vent. I was so happy to see that my best friend was still here with us. It was late so I decided to go home so that I could prepare for work to tomorrow.

During Kamara's hospital stay Karli lived with me and became my responsibility. Being that she was my god daughter it was only right that I did. Karli was a very smart little girl and aware of everything that had occurred. She was also proud to be her mother's hero and saved her life. Karli was also sad and confused about losing her father and being a witness to him trying to kill her mother. Lil Dave was pronounced dead on the scene when the paramedics arrived. Although Lil Dave tried to kill Kamara, Karli still loved and missed her father. Could you believe that his family put up a big fuss about Karli not being at the funeral? I was not going to allow her to be around those people. I don't care if they didn't have anything to do with what happened. It's just over the years they sat back not giving a damn about Karli and they didn't like Kamara. Fuck them and their feelings. My main concern was my best friend Kamara and to make sure that she was receiving the necessary treatment that she needed to heal. We all have to be there for her so that she could recuperate and bounce back stronger than before. With the help of Keith, he made sure that Kamara's transitioning from the hospital to her new home was easy. Keith remained to keep a straight face but deep down he was really taking it hard. He blamed himself for not killing Keith in the beginning, feeling that it would've never happened if he did. I told Keith that he didn't do anything wrong and that it was meant for Lil Dave to die that way and not meant for

Kamara to die at all. Right now we all just needed to focus on the future. Tee was by my side during all of this. Now that I was responsible for Karli he and I didn't really spend a lot of naughty time together. Whenever I got the chance to get away with him I did. Today Karli was spending time with Emani and her children. I had to knock out some major grocery shopping and shopping in general. I went to Walmart in Forest Park to do my shopping. Tee called and told me that he was heading toward my way and to call him after I was done shopping. By the time that I was finished I had two shopping carts filled to capacity with food and personal items. Karli was small but her little ass could eat all day if you let her. The snotty cashier rung up my items and I got the hell out of there. I placed everything in the trunk and was ready to head home so that I could finally meet up with my hubby Tee. As I drove through the parking lot it felt like my car was dragging. When it started jerking on me I pulled over to an empty area of the parking lot. Upon stepping out I seen that my car started smoking. I grabbed my purse and cellphone quickly and stepped out of my car. The smelly and thick smoke was coming out of the exhaust into the air making it hard for me to see. I stepped back and one moment later my car was on fire and exploded.

Poof!!! "What the fuck!" I was knocked to the ground by the force of the pressure. Frantically I called Tee to tell him what the hell just happened as people watched and exited from their vehicles.

Nearby

I sat back and watched the bitch car in flames. My mission was somewhat accomplished, didn't quite go exactly as I planned. The plan was to blow that bitch up as well. All that got damn work that I put into this. It took a while for me to catch up with the bitch and place the prescription filled bottle of Drano inside her gas tank. My plan was to get rid of her just like I did Shay. I don't know where Tee finds them women from but he wasn't going to be able to flaunt his hoes around me so freely. I worked too hard to secure my spot in his life. Without me Tee and his crew would never as big as they are. The crowd was starting to grow as everyone watched the fire department and the police arrive. She was crying as they placed her on the stretcher and examined her. Moments later Tee pulled into the parking lot as they were putting his thot bitch into the ambulance. That was my cue to get out of there, I feared that he would see me. I had no business being on this side of town at this hood ass Walmart at that. I blended in with the traffic as the police directed everyone out of the parking lot. The police allowed Tee to go over to the ambulance to see about her. She fell into his arms crying being dramatic and shit. Looking at Tee console her made me want to throw the fuck up. Oh bitch please cry me a mother fucking river. She better thank God that she is still alive because that certainly wasn't a part of the plan. I rolled out of the vicinity before my cover was blown. Hopefully Ty would take heed to the information that I provided him. I was ready to set Tee ass up since he has stop being involved with me and cut me off completely. I know that sending Ty and his crew off on Tee is a ruthless and cut throat thing for me to. He played me, yes he threw me a few bucks, bought my pretty white Benz C class drop top, and purchased my condo. But I needed more of him and unlimited cash. At this point in my life I was too old to be sitting back and watching him flaunt around another bitch in my face. That shit was foul and mad disrespectful how he just cut me off. Tee wasn't going to fuck me over and just drop me whenever he felt like it. The last time that I tried to reach out to him he had a new number. I reached out to Keith and the Twins, but that was a waste of time because they weren't fucking with my ass either. That just added fuel to the fire and made me more upset.

Meantime

The paramedics rushed me to Loyola Hospital immediately. When I hit the pavement I had a few bumps and bruises but nothing major. Tee was there with me at the hospital while they performed x rays on me. When I returned back to the emergency room Tee was waiting on me. Seeing him here let me know how much he truly cared about me. I was still shaken up about everything.

"Are you okay? Tell me what happened?" Tee asked.

"All I did was get into the car, started it up and as I was driving my car was jerking and smoking. I get out and then Boom! It catches on fire, no I'm not good. I could've been fucked up or even worse dead if I would've remained inside the car." I started crying.

"Don't cry you're here and alive. In the meantime let's make sure that you cool. Is the pain medicine working? I don't want you to feel any pain, just relax." Tee kissed me on my forehead.

He pulled out his phone and made a phone call, excused himself and stepped out in the hall to talk. I was trying to hear what he was talking about but couldn't really hear him. My car blowing up scared the fuck out of me. The blood pressure cuff on my arm pumped up squeezing the life out of my arm. When it was done my blood pressure read 180/100. I wasn't surprised that my blood pressure was up being that I just was moments away from death. I relaxed like Tee said and tried to gather all my thoughts together. Everything inside my car was gone, the food, a few things that I had in my trunk, and hell I didn't have a vehicle anymore. It was cool because I had full coverage with State Farm. I closed my eyes and tried to get some rest but I couldn't relax hospitals and I don't get along. Moments later my parents rushed into the small emergency room.

"Oh my God Tichina what happened?" My mother said worried but happy to see me.

I told my mother and father what happened and they started praying and thanking God for covering me. Tee stood behind them and watched as they carried on.

"Excuse me mom and dad, this is Tavion. My friend that I told you about." I pointed to Tee and he stepped up to shake my father hand and gave my mother a hug.

I was surprise to see that the meet and greet between them went great. My mother smiled and winked at me as Tee and my father spoke man to man. I smiled, I knew that Tee was mature and could handle my parents. It was just that I haven't introduced a man to parents in years. The doctor came in and said that everything was fine, but that they wanted to keep me overnight for observation. There was no way that I was staying overnight here alone. Tee wasn't going to leave me alone in the hospital. He had to go and make a run to handle some business before it got too late. When everyone finally left I tried to watch some television. The news was on and my car explosion made the news. At that moment I remembered about Karli and started searching my phone. After the accident I called my parents and placed my phone inside my purse. When I finally got my phone I seen that I had at least thirty missed calls from Emani. Somehow my phone was on vibrate, maybe I accidently pushed the side button on my iPhone. I called Emani and told her everything that happened and that I will be released tomorrow. She was cool and I made her promise not to tell Karli. That poor baby has already been through enough shit already. I spoke with Karli on the phone to make sure that she was fine with spending the night over Emani house. She said that she was having fun but was ready to go. I had to think of something quick to come up with. Fuck! The last thing that I wanted to do was make her stay some place where she didn't want to. Maybe I could have my mother go over to pick her up. No I can't do that, she hasn't had any younger children around her in years. Karli started crying for me to come and get here. I had no other choice but to leave so I told her that I will be to get her soon. I called Tee and told him that I was signing out because Karli was crying for me to come and get her. Tee didn't argue with me and said okay as long as I was fine. I press the call button, the nurse came in.

"I'm sorry but I have to leave, although I know that the doctor wanted me to stay overnight." I politely said.

"Miss Jefferson under doctor's advice we need to keep an eye on you until the morning." The young nurse said.

"I know what the doctor said, but I have no one to watch my God daughter. I really need to be home with her."

"Let me page the doctor to get permission from him. I will be back after he notifies me."

This hospital has me twisted. I started getting dressed preparing to go home. I was leaving rather or not the doctor allowed me to. I knew that Tee will be back to me soon and I needed to be ready. My cellphone was blowing up from different people checking on me. Some of those people that I didn't know still had my number. I guess seeing my story on the news made me popular. Tee walked into the room while I was putting on my Air Max's.

"You ready to go baby? Tee helped me get up.

"No I have to wait for the nurse."

The young nurse must have known that I was ready to go. She walked back in with paperwork for me to sign and prescriptions that I had to fill. Tee and I walked out the hospital and got into his car. It hit me when I realized that I didn't have a car. How was going to get back and forth to work. I called Emani and told her to have Karli ready and that I would be there in twenty minutes. I grabbed the ride side of my head, my head was starting to hurt. Tee noticed that and turned the music down.

"You cool? Maybe you should take something for pain. Let's put your prescription in and then on the way back after Karli it should be ready. He stopped off at Walgreens and rode through the drive thru to drop off my prescription.

The pharmacy technician told us that it would be ready in forty five minutes. That was perfect since we had to pick up Karli. When I pulled up in front of Emani's house I called her.

"You can send Karli out. I'm in front of your house sitting in a silver Jaguar." I said.

Emani walked Karli out to the car. Karli was so happy to see me and climbed in the back seat. She was happy to see Tee as well.

"Are you okay? When your mother called me I didn't believe it. Was it a factory defect or something with your car? I'm just happy that you didn't hurt." Emani said as she gave me a hug.

When she hugged me I whispered in her ear. "I don't want Karli to know." Emani caught on and we continued to talk in code so that Karli wouldn't catch onto what we were talking about. Emani spoke to Tee before she told me that she loved me and returned to go back in the house. Ty came out on the porch and waved at me as Emani stepped back into the house. I waved back and Tee pulled off. Now I was hungry with a headache. All my food was blown up with the car. We picked up my medication and grabbed some food to eat. Karli was so happy to be back with me and didn't have a clue as to what had happened. We got settled in and I sat her in front of the television with her food and turned on the Nickelodeon channel. Tee and I went into my bedroom for some privacy.

"Tee thank you for being here for me. Damn I still can't believe that I was damn near gone. Just like that I could've been dead." I started crying, Tee held me in his arms. "Now I have to call State Farm to file a claim. How am I going to get back and forth to work now?"

"Don't worry about that. You can drive my Porsche Truck until you find out what they're going to do about your car. In the meantime get you some rest. I have to see about getting you some food in here today."

Tee made a phone call while I went to go run me some hot water. My body was aching so badly from hitting the concrete. He walked into the bedroom and told me that he was about to meet up with Keith and will be back. Tee made sure that Karli and I was straight before he left. I was cool and soaking in my bath water.

Four hours later Tee was calling my phone. I was knocked out in bed with Karli snuggled up next to me. Her little butt had climbed in bed with me instead of going into the other bedroom. I smiled and answered my phone.

177

"Hello." I said in my sleepy voice.

"I'm about to pull up in a minute. Make sure that you decent, I got Keith and the twins with me." Tee said on the phone.

"Okay."

I got up to brush my teeth and threw on something more appropriate. I closed the door to my bedroom when I heard Tee ring my doorbell. I didn't want them to wake up Karli. Tee, Keith and the Twins walked inside carrying bags of food. They all asked me how I was doing and gave me hug after they placed the bags in the kitchen.

Tee gave me a hug and a kiss. "I hope that I picked out the things that you and Karli would like. That food should last you both for a month. Here is the keys to my Porsche truck, until they issue you a rental and you find out what's going on with your car. It's parked out front and filled up."

"Thanks babe, you're the best ever." I gave him a big kiss jumping into his arms. His friends laughed at us, calling us corny. We ignored them, "I swear if they weren't with you I would take you down right now." I whispered in his ear.

"Your little hot ass always trying to take me down." Tee laughed.

We both started laughing because he wasn't lying. I was the aggressive one in the bedroom. Maybe because I have so much built inside of me. Tee brought out the sexual beast in me, we both matched one another in the bedroom. Although I was aching I still wanted to be tapped and release some of this stress. We walked in the front room so that I could walk them out the door. I had to be at work tomorrow and deal with my insurance company. Karli had to get dropped off at summer camp so I had to get an early start.

Chapter 15

Emani

After Tichina and Tee pulled off I went back inside the house with Ty following behind me. I don't know why he came on the front porch in the first place. He was trying to be nosy like always, maybe Tee's Jaguar caught his attention. I went upstairs to my bedroom when Ty came walking into the room. Ty had a suspicious look in his eyes, I knew that look to well. He was on some bullshit and was ready to be changed. He sat next to me on the bed smiling and shit. I rolled my eyes.

"Why you rolling your eyes and looking at me like that for?" Ty laughed and joked.

"Because you're on some bullshit. Why are you being nice to me all of a sudden?" I looked at him with slanted eyes.

"Was that the nigga Tee with Tichina?" Ty came straight out with the bullshit.

"Yes it was him Ty."

"He looks familiar, like I've seen him from somewhere before." Ty said.

"Yes that's the infamous Tee. It's not going to be easy to get to him Ty."

"What you saying, you think them niggas can't be touched?" Ty asked getting serious.

"No they can't not unless you come on with it. Besides they're not easy to touch."

"With the help of you I could get closer to them all you have to do is continue to keep on questioning Tichina. Pretty soon she would budge you just have to around her more and play things off." Ty said.

"It's easier said than done. Especially when she's always with him. With Kamara being in the hospital we haven't been spending too much time together."

"You'll get your chance real soon. I promise we will hit them niggas so fast that they wouldn't see us coming."

I just remained quiet, Ty was so anxious about getting at Tee all of a sudden. I wonder who put him on to Tee. Maybe it was Jabari being that he is from Englewood and pretty much knows about them Southside niggas. Ty was putting me in the middle of his bullshit once again. Trying to get Tichina to tell me anything about Tee was hard. Tichina never really did share certain things with me. She is a lot closer with Kamara when it comes to certain topics. It hasn't always been like that, it started when I got with Ty. I didn't care and never let it bother me but I promise to never betray my friends. Technically Tee isn't a friend of mine so that doesn't count. Besides he's not going to be with Tichina for too long anyway. Tichina never keeps a man because of her bad attitude that runs them away. I was caught between helping my man and crossing my friend.

Wednesday after work I decided to spend some time with Tichina. I made sure to call her before I popped up at her house. Honestly I wanted to see how she was doing after the car explosion. I just didn't feel comfortable with setting my friend up. I'm just going to lie to Ty and tell him that I can't get any information out of her. When I arrived at her house I noticed a Porsche truck parked out front. That bitch was nice I wonder who truck it was. Tichina was in the house cooking Shrimp Alfredo and Crab Legs.

"Damn friend I came right on time I see." I said loudly coming through the door.

I gave Karli a hug and Tichina as well. I sat my new Berkin bag down on her dining room table.

"Girl I've been cooking everyday now since I've been dealing with Tee. All he does is eat all day long." Tichina said.

"Girl who truck is that parked in front of your house? Is someone dipping off around here with them girls who stay in that court way building?"

"No that's Tee truck, he's letting me drive it until I find out what my insurance company is going to do about my car. Right now they are investigating the claim."

"That's cool, so Tee is really your man I see. I'm so happy for you about damn time you getting some D on the regular." I put on a phony smile and laughed.

As Tichina ran her mouth I became interested waiting on a moment when I could invite myself to hang out with them. Tichina wasn't never going to invite so I had to think of an excuse to hang around them.

"Girl that twin Justin is cute, hook me up girl." I said.

Tichina stopped and looked at me in shock. "No way, I don't have time to fall out with Ty ass. If you want to holler at Justin you better do it yourself."

"Okay I will do whenever the next time I see him. A real friend would hook me up though, but hey I understand if you don't want to be in the middle of anything."

"Enough about Tee and his friends. I went to hospital earlier, they moved Kamara to the rehabilitation department. She's doing well and if she keeps it up she will be home by the end of the month." Tichina said.

"That's great! I really miss Kamara and I promise that I will go visit her soon." Now I was telling the truth about that.

"You better because you've been slacking on being a good friend. Kamara asked about you today. You need to be trying to go see her ASAP." Tichina was serious.

I knew that I haven't been up there as much as Tichina to see about her. I changed the subject before we started arguing. The last thing that I wanted to do was fall out about something that I was wrong about. Tichina showed off some of the gifts that Tee bought her over the week. It was expensive clothes, shoes, and even an Apple Macbook.

While Tichina showed off her new items I noticed the wad of cash sitting on her dresser. It was a stack of one hundred dollar bills. I know that Tichina didn't have it like that. Tee was really spoiling the shit out of my friend. Damn I guess he really does fuck with her heavy. Apart of me felt envious, not because she was getting spoiled. I was envious because it was happening so fast and unbelievable.

"Girl you better count your blessings because it's not too many men like Tee left out here. I'm genuinely happy for you." I sat on Tichina's bed watching her as she showed me her new things.

I wished that I was in her shoes right about now. Damn Ty needs to step his mother fucking game up. Real mother fucking quick!

The next day I went up to the hospital to visit Kamara. When I arrived she was sitting in her chair looking out the window.

"Surprised!" I said happily as I walked into her room. I gave her the lovely vase of orchids and a card.

"Thank you Emani, they're very lovely." She read the card and then gave me a hug.

"You're welcome, I know that they are your favorite. I'm sorry for not coming to see you more often. I'm here now and promise to support you more. You look good, how do you feel?" I asked.

"I'm feeling fine just sitting here admiring my view. I'm so ready to go home. I miss Karli so much. What have you been up to Emani?"

"Girl just working and staying in the house. You know I'm not about to be partying when you're going through this. I've just been spending time with my children. It's so much killing going on out here the safest place to be is in the house. I just been staying out of the way."

"That's good to hear, but you seem kind of tense. You know Emani we have been friends for over twenty years. I could tell when something is going on with you. What's really going on E?" Kamara looked into my eyes.

"You know me and Ty are still having problems. I'm just trying to keep my household together. The last thing that I need is a broken family." I lied and tried to blame victim.

"Hmmmm, what time is it? They should be coming to get me for physical therapy soon. Are you going to stick around?" Kamara asked me totally blowing off what I just said.

As soon as I was about to speak someone knocked on the door to transport her to physical therapy.

"Yes I don't mind coming with you."

I watched Kamara get up and walk for the first time when I came to visit her. She had to use a walker but she was doing really well. The fire had damaged some nerves in her legs that made it hard for her to walk. The physical therapist was very patient and polite with her. Kamara was finished an hour later. We went back to her room and had lunch. I ordered some food and had it delivered to the hospital. I really loved Kamara like she was my sister. I helped her go the bathroom even though she didn't want me to. Before you know it I was up there for five hours. I didn't want to leave her but I had to go see about my children. I gave her a hug and told her how much that I loved her. With everything that was happening around me I knew that tomorrow wasn't never promised. I made it home to a fucked up house. Shit was everywhere, I promise Ty wasn't worth shit. Ty and his friends were busy kicking it that he didn't care what the children did. I was pissed off and ready to go off on Ty ass.

"Ty!!!!!" I yelled from the top of the stairs. I could hear Ty tell his company to leave.

He marched up the stairs. "What you doing all that yelling for?"

"Do you see my got damn house?" My children were quietly hiding in their rooms now. My baby girl Tyeisha was sleeping in our bed. Ty was so fucking irresponsible, the only fucking thing that he cared about was money, money, money. I was so overwhelmed and tired of a lot of his bullshit. He started cleaning up the mess that he sons made, because I damn sure wasn't going to do it. I just laughed, sometimes you have to laugh to keep from going the fuck off. I laid across my bed scrolling through my Instagram page not paying Ty any attention. The last time that I was on social media was the time when Sunshine was killed. I see that I didn't miss out on nothing but just some stunting. My text alert went off on my phone letting me know that I had a message. It was from Tichina, she sent me a video to watch. I clicked on the video to watch it. Tichina was at a car lot, behind her it a white 2014 Range Rover with a big red bow on it. Tichina got behind the wheel crying and kissing Tee. As I watched the video a call came through.

"Did you see the video? Girl Tee got me a Range Rover bitch! I'm so happy. I love my baby so much!" Tichina was excited and happy as hell.

"Yes that's so sweet of him. What ever happened with your insurance claim?"

"Oh girl that's another story for another day. I'm about to pull off now so I will call you back tomorrow. Girl I'm about to fuck the shit out of Tee."

"You better get on that boo. I love your new truck and talk to you tomorrow."

After I ended the call with Tichina I replayed the video over again. I wanted that truck so bad that I was thinking about trading in my Jeep Cherokee for it. I was going to wait till next year to flip it around tax time. Now I had to sit back and watch my best friend ride around in the truck that I wanted. Ty came into the room and went inside the closet. I jumped up quickly to show him the video of Tichina's new whip, but I was really trying to see what he was doing. He was placing money into the safe that we had hidden in our closet.

"Check this video out bae." I pushed my phone in his face, he had no other choice but to view it.

Ty looked at the video and smirked. "So that nigga Tee bought her a new whip. That's cool, did you find out any information yet?"

"Not yet but I'm working on it. I'm trying to set something up with her, him and his friends. The only way that I can find out anything is if I'm only around. I could only go off what I see. If you want this to work without the finger being pointed at me, it's going to take time."

"Cool you need to start working on that. I don't care if you have to fuck one of his friends, do what you have to do. I've been doing my homework on them niggas. I'll be patient but we ready to make a move when we know where to go and who to hit."

"I'm working on it bae, you can count on me."

I kissed Ty and sucked on his lower bottom lip. At first I wasn't down with setting up my bestie man, but seeing that new Range that she just got made me jealous. Now I had to put on a phony role whenever I was around, acting like I was really happy for her. When we hit Tee he isn't even going to expect it. I wanted to know where he laid his head at and more importantly where was the money at. Ty threw me across the bed, pulling out my breast and sucked on them roughly. We didn't care that our daughter was sleeping in the bed.

"You got your man back baby? You not going to let your man down are you?" Ty pumped inside of me making me moan. His dick was so good that I agreed to anything that he said.

"Yes baby I have your back. Oh God please don't stop, yes fuck me like you love me." I dug my nails deeply into his back.

I love Ty and willing to do whatever it takes to see the both of us grow into a power couple.

Chapter 16

Kamara

Today was a very important day for me. Everyone gathered in my hospital room surrounded around me. All of the medical professionals along with Tichina, Tee, Keith, a few of my family members and my baby girl Karli. I was so happy to finally be released from the hospital. They were happy for me as well. This past month for me was rigorous one, but I was a true fighter and wasn't going to lose. I had a lot to live for, Karli needed me the most and I was not going to let her down. Everyone gave and expressed their love for me. I smiled and thank all of the medical staff for being patient with me. I know that I was a handful but it was the pain talking not me. Karli sat on my lap while Tichina pushed me in the wheelchair out the door. Keith helped me get inside of his truck. On the way home I just sat back and enjoyed the ride. I asked Keith to turn off the air so that I could roll down the window. I preferred the fresh air instead, it felt good to be reunited with Karli. She was in the back seat singing to Rhianna new song. We pulled into my garage, with Tichina and Tee following behind us. Emani's Jeep Cherokee was parked outside in front of my home. Keith helped me get out, Karli grabbed my hand.

"Mommy we have a surprise for you." She was so excited that her tiny self-tried to drag me into the house.

"You do baby girl, well I'm excited to find out."

We all walked into my home, it was my first time being back since after I purchased it.

"Surprise!!!!" Karli screamed when we walked inside.

Emani was standing in my dining room with her children, behind her was a table covered with food. It was a fest and looked like it was catered. Placing my hands over my mouth the only thing that I could was cry. There was balloons and a banner hanging on the wall that said welcome home. Karli was laughing and enjoying the moment.

"Do you like it?" Keith kissed me on my cheek.

"Yes, all of this for me?" I cried.

"You deserve this and more baby." Keith said,

Emani's children gave a big hug, I was so happy to see them. I was in the hospital for two months. One month I was hospitalized and the second month I was in rehabilitation. The summer was practically over with, it came and left.

"Thank you everyone for being here for me. I wouldn't know what I would do without any of you. Now I'm hungry so let's eat." I wiped away my tears and took a seat at the table.

Tichina prayed over the food and I dug in. The macaroni and cheese was like heaven in my mouth. No more tasteless, nasty hospital food. Everyone was really happy that I was at home. We all chilled out at my place, catching up with everything that happened for the last two months. By six pm my house was empty, Keith and I were alone. Karli was upstairs in her room enjoying a movie. She was so in love with her bedroom, it was decorated in her favorite color purple. Now that Keith and I could really talk I had to thank him.

"I want to thank you for making sure that my transition from the hospital to home was all good. I was worried about moving after I got it. You have no idea how much weight you lifted off of me." I looked around my place, everything was perfect.

"You know I got your back. I told you that as long as you're with me that you don't have to worry about nothing. With the help of your friends and Karli we made sure that you would be comfortable once you stepped out of the hospital."

"So I'm with you now, it's me and you Keith? No other women, dips, crazy ex-girlfriends, or fans? I just need to make sure because before the situation occurred we were friends with benefits."

"Yes we're officially together. When you were in the hospital I felt like I never wanted to leave your side. My feelings for you grew stronger day by day. You made me feel some type of way inside."

Keith and I talked about our new journey that we were about to start together. Although we were in a relationship we weren't going to live together just yet. He did however plan on staying overnight at times. When that happened I wanted to make him feel as though he was at home. After going two months without any dick I was more than ready to hop on his. We worked our way upstairs, before I got shit started I had to check on Karli. She was sleeping peacefully in her queen size bed. My daughter had a big girl room, a big difference from the small bedroom that you could barely fit anything into. I kissed her softly because I didn't want to disturb her beauty rest. Keith ran me some bath water, something that I missed the most. I just wanted to soak all the pain away that I went through. He washed my back gently with a soap filled sponge. I blew some bubbles and splashed some water on him a few times. Keith splashed me back so I pulled him in the jacuzzi with me. We were laughing too hard, it's been so long since I've laughed. We got out of the water and I wrapped my body quickly with the towel and hopped in the bed. I was trying to cover up my body. I still felt uncomfortable about the scars on my body. Keith took noticed to that and pulled the cover off me. I grabbed the cover from him but he wouldn't let go of it.

"Why are you trying to cover yourself up?" Keith grew frustrated throwing the blanket onto the floor.

"My scars, they're hideous." I started to cry while rubbing the scars on my legs and arms.

"You're beautiful, very beautiful. I don't love you any less because of your scars."

He pushed my hands away and started kissing on my scars. His kisses made my clit jumped. I wanted him inside of me. Keith handle me gently, "It is okay you can be rough." I whispered in his ear.

His rock hard dick felt the inside of my pussy like it was a perfect match. Keith threw my thick thighs on his shoulders going deeper. I felt his dick in my stomach, I had to catch my breath. As he went deeper I couldn't hold it inside as hit all the right spots.

"Ohhhhhhh! Keith I miss you so much babe."

Keith couldn't hold it in much longer. "Ugggggggg! He moaned collapsing on top of me. "You got some good shit down there." He rolled over lying next to me out of breath.

"I love you Keith, please don't ever leave me." I softly said as I looked into his eyes.

"I love you sexy, don't worry I got you from here on out. You and Karli are very important to me." I started crying. "Stop crying beautiful everything will be alright, you straight." Keith held me in his arms. For the first time I felt protected by a real man.

Over the weeks I've been pretty much just chilling at home and spending time with Karli and Keith. Tichina and Emani was hanging out a lot more and would come by and hang out with me every chance they got. I was busy trying to catch up on my favorite television series Scandal when my doorbell rang. I looked out the window and seen Tichina's Range Rover parked in my driveway.

"Girl what brings you by?" Tichina had three bags in her hand. "What is that you have?" I asked her trying to take a peek in the bags. "Smells good."

Tichina removed her shoes and stepped into my house placing the bags on my dining room table. "I stopped Priscilla's on the way over here and grabbed some soul food."

"Yes right on time because I didn't feel like cooking at all." I called Karli to tell her to come get some food. She was happy to Tichina and more than happier that she brought food.

We all sat down and ate our food. After Karli was finished she went back to her room. Tichina didn't waste any time spilling the news. She told me that she and Emani have been spending a lot of time together with Tee and Jay. Supposedly Emani is talking to Jay now, which I was surprised to hear. As long as I've known Emani she has never cheated on Ty before. I wonder what was up with that arrangement. Hearing about all the fun that they have been having made me feel as though I was missing out on all the fun. I wish that Keith and I could join them but I wasn't ready to get back out there yet.

"Sounds like you have been having a lot of fun. Hearing that Emani is talking to Jay seems kind of funny to me." I looked at Tichina sideways.

"You know I felt the same way as well. Maybe she felt as though she didn't want to seem like the third wheel all the time."

"So what they call themselves creeping because both of them are in a relationship. I don't know about this Tichina, you don't want to be caught in the middle if Shay finds out."

"Look I didn't have anything to do with them hooking up. They're both two adults that made that decision on their own. If anything goes down I have nothing to do with it."

Tichina is so clueless but I see straight through Emani's disguise. She only wants to fuck around with Jay because of his money. Emani was money hungry and was willing to do anything for it. She wasn't always that way, being with Ty has rubbed off on her in a bad way.

199

The next weekend I met up with Emani to discuss some things. Instead of stuffing my mouth I was working out. I waited for her at the gym so that we could work out. I picked up ten pounds that I had to get rid of. Emani walked in, I waved to her so that she could join me. I was warming up walking around the track before I hit the elliptical machine. Emani and I did two laps and chatted about our children. I wasn't trying to talk about know damn kids I wanted to know what was her agenda with dealing with Jay. We went over to the punching bags and put on our boxing gloves

"So you and Jay fucking around now? When have you ever been someone's side chick before?" Emani had a dumb look on her face. She wasn't expecting me to ask her that question?

"Girl for the record I'm nobody's side chick." She punched the gym bag. "Jay and I are just friends that's all. Why do you care so much about what I'm doing? Emani rolled her eyes.

"Don't roll your eyes at me. You know damn well if Ty finds out he will fuck you up. That's not a good look for you or us. We're never someone's second choice, never.

Tichina and I have something real with Tee and Keith and we don't need you to fuck that up for us."

"Trust me I won't break up ya'll happy relationships." Emani's cellphone rang, she stopped talking to answer it. "Hey Jay baby what's up? I'm at the gym working out with Kamara. Sure dinner sounds like fun, see you tonight at seven." She ended the call, "Now back to what we were talking about again."

"You better be careful and watch yourself. If some shit goes down you are on your own. Don't look for me or Tichina to have your back. I don't know what has gotten into you but you're making me despise you. Be careful because at the end of it all, you'll be the only one hurt."

"I'm a big girl, I know what I'm doing. What Jay and I do is Jay and I our business. I will make sure that it doesn't interfere with you and Keith, okay." Emani and I stood face to face like we were about to fight.

"Get the fuck out of my face before you be picking your teeth up off the ground." I said through clenched teeth.

"I'm out of here. Kamara I don't want to fight you." Emani took off her boxing gloves and threw them down on the floor. She laughed and marched out of the gym.

"Shiesty bitch!" I said under my breath.

I don't know what the hell Emani was up to, but I was onto her ass. I bet money that Emani was on some bullshit, I can smell it.

Chapter 17

Emani

The bitch Kamara is on to me, but that wasn't going to stop me from pursuing my mission. Tonight I was going on my date with Jay so that I could get this thing rolling. How dare Kamara tell me who I can and can't fuck with! She's not my fucking momma, hell my own mother can't even tell me what to do. I drove to Woodfield Mall so that I could do some retail shopping. I had to look good tonight for my date. Jay was paid and if he played his cards right tonight he was going to get laid. Hell Ty haven't been hitting right lately anyway, I had to get some dick from somewhere. Kamara was right about one thing and that was, I was no one's side chick. This was a new role for me and I was going to play the hell out of it. I stopped off into Bloomingdale's to buy myself a sexy dress, an elegant clutch, and a pair of new sling backs. After that I swung by Victoria's Secret to purchased me some lingerie just in case I was getting freaky tonight. While I was trying on different pieces I received a phone call from Tichina.

"What the hell is going on with you? I just got off the phone with Kamara." Tichina barked in my ear.

"First of all you need to stop yelling in my ear. Second ain't shit wrong with me, she's the one with the problem." I said in my defense.

"Well she made some valid points about you messing with Jay. What is this I hear about you and him going out tonight?"

"Tichina please don't play dumb with me. You didn't have a problem when I was hanging on Jay arm all last week. Why are you surprised to hear that I'm going on a date tonight with him?"

"Look I'm not going to tell you what or who to do. Just don't get your feelings involved and fuck up what you have going on at home. As a matter of fact fuck that bullshit, do you. But in the meantime you need to call Kamara and apologize to her."

"You got me fucked up if you think that's going to happen. If anything she needs to be apologizing to me. Let me get off this phone, I'm at Woodfield Mall inside Victoria Secret's dressing room loud as hell. I will call you back when I leave out." I hung up the phone.

Tichina blew me because she was always taking up for Kamara. I was happy with the items that I tried on so I decided to get everything. I put back on my clothes and stepped out of the dressing room. I looked at the time on my Apple watch and seen that I had several text messages from Ty. Maybe I didn't get them because of the bad reception in the dressing room. The checkout line was pretty long and the cashier didn't make it any better as she talked on the phone. A few seconds later another woman came to help her with the long line. As I got closer to the counter the woman on the phone whispered something to the cashier before she rung me up. My total for my items were four hundred dollars. When it was time for me to pay the cashier gave me a hard time. She was asking me questions but I had an answer for every questioned that she asked. I purchased the items and got out of there. I walked through Bloomingdales and exited out the same door with my keys in my hand. I felt someone watching me as soon as the automatic door opened. My instinct told me to look over my shoulder and when I did mall security was approaching me.

"Young lady please stop!" The white male security guard said.

I made a break for it knocking down anyone that was in my path. I weaved in and out the parking lot leaving the security guards behind me. I hit the automatic starter on my car and was one foot away from it. Ducking down I hid behind a Chrysler Pacifica and watched the guards talk on their walkie talkies. "We lost her, be on the lookout out for and African American female, with a ponytail and that's wearing hot pink and black workout clothes." The black security guard was getting closer to me. Suddenly a white teenage boy looked at me hiding behind the Chrysler. He spoke up, my heart start racing as the black guard was two cars away from. "I think I seen her run over that way." The white teenage boy said throwing off the security guard. "Thanks." He ran off toward the opposite way in the parking lot.

"You need to get in your car and go now." The white teenage boy said as he looked out for me.

"Thank you so much!" I dashed off and jumped in my car pulling out and blending in with the vehicles. I had a white Bebe shirt in my front seat so I threw it on and pulled the ponytail holder out of my head. My luxury tresses fell down my back. What was so crazy was that I still had my shopping bags. I hide them under the items that were in my back seat and drove off toward Higgins Road.

Meanwhile

When Tichina called Emani she had me on three way and told me to be quiet. Normally we didn't do the secret three way calling, but today was necessary. Tichina didn't believe it when I told her that Emani and I had some words. I became upset when I heard that she was shopping for some lingerie. I knew that she was buying something to wear tonight when she was with Jay. After I got off the phone with Tichina I took it upon myself to drop the dime on her ass. I called up to Victoria Secret and told them that they had a professional card cracker in their store shopping and gave them a description of Emani. Hopefully they apprehended her hoe ass and she was being shipped on her way to jail. As of now Emani and I was not on speaking terms period. She wasn't being herself, it's like someone else has jumped into her body. By us being friends for so long we all knew one another down to the tee. Trust me Emani was on some slick shit and when it all boils down to it I will not be involved. Tichina can deal with her if she wants to, but if she was smart she would cut that bitch off too. Anyway enough about that snake ass bitch. Keith was on his way to come see me. Karli was chilling with Tichina today so we had the house to ourselves for some hours. I showered and waited for him naked in bed like he requested. Since Keith and I been exclusive I made a set of keys for him. He and Tichina were the only two people who had keys to my place. Keith arrived and we started fucking all over the house. It was only right that we bless my new house.

"Emani didn't you see me blowing up your phone? I've been calling your ass for the last hour." Ty was waiting on me at the front door. I walked past him totally ignoring his ass and went straight to the bathroom to turn on the shower. I was musty, sweaty, and hot after working out and running from the guards. "Do you hear me?" Ty barked in my ear. I leaned over the bathroom sink and took a look at him in the bathroom mirror ready to snap out on his ass. "What the hell is up with you?'

"Ty I almost got caught inside Woodfield Mall and had to take a dash out of there."

"Damn that's fucked up. You have to be cool out there in the burbs. I keep trying to tell your ass that you be doing too much and have to slow down."

I got in the shower and let the water knock off the funk. Ty went away to talk a phone call in private. When I got out I was ear hustling on his conversation. From what I heard they were going to hit someone up. Ty seen that I was listening and started talking in code. "You don't have to talk in code around me." I plopped down on the bed next to him. He ended the phone call. "I have a date tonight with Jay." I applied lotion to my body and sprayed perfume in between my legs making sure that my pussy was Flower Bomb fresh.

"Damn you getting prepared aren't you? Where are you going?" From the look on Ty face I can see that he was starting to feel a little jealous.

"I'm just doing what you ask me to do. I'm not sure where he's taking me, it's a surprise." I pulled out the royal blue lingerie set to put on.

"That's good our plan is working out great! Do what you got to do to get whatever information out of him."

"Yes Mr I will do whatever it takes."

Ty kissed me on the neck smiling. That's fucked that he didn't care about me anymore. He was willing to send his woman off on another nigga just to come up. I was foolish to even agree with this bullshit. As I looked in the mirror I was starting to have second thoughts about meeting up with Jay. The greedy, money hungry person in me was telling me not to cancel and to get up with him.

I pulled up in front of the John Hancock Building and paid the valet attendant to park my car. When I walked in Jay was already there. He looked smiling, flashing his pearly white teeth. I gave him a hug and got a whiff of the Creed cologne. He pulled out my chair and I took a seat.

"You look beautiful in your blue." Jay said with lust in his eyes.

"Thank you, you look very handsome in your all black." I smiled.

Jay didn't waste any time rubbing on my thigh. I didn't stop him because that shit felt good. We ordered a drink and our food as we converse. Our date was going by fast but I was enjoying it.

"Look Emani you know that I have a woman and you have a nigga so let's just fuck and get it over with."

Damn Jay was blunt but I don't blame him because I wanted to fuck just like him. "I'm down for whatever. You don't have to tell me twice." I licked my lips and flicked my tongue exposing my tongue ring.

Jay asked for the check and we got out of there. He told me to follow me to his place. From our previous conversations I knew that his woman Shay didn't live with him. Jay lived in Tinley Park. As I followed him I called Ty letting him know what was up.

"Ty I'm going back to his place. He lives in Tinley Park alone. I will text you the address when I pull up." Ty had so many damn demands.

"Hey if you have to fuck that nigga I don't care. Just keep his ass occupied till I get there." Ty ordered.

"Okay, look he's calling me I have to go."

We pulled up in front of his eleven thousand square foot home. Jay and I walked inside and got right into it. Jay popped half an ex pill and I popped the other half. He poured me some Belaire Rose and drank the rest from the bottle.

"Turn on some music so I can dance for you." Jay turned on some Future, the champagne had made feeling free. I removed my lingerie and started twerking for him. He watched me pop and clap my ass as he stroked his hard dick. Jay had a big ass dick, two times the size of Ty's dick. I slowed it down a bit and crawled my way to him. I took all of Jay's dick in my mouth, slurping and swallowing it up. Jay pushed his dick deeper down my throat causing me to cry and gag.

"Yes hoe get all this dick down your throat." He pumped in and out of my mouth fucking it. "Turn that phat ass around." I did what he requested, he smacked me on my ass. He opened up my ass cheeks and ate my pussy and ass. I moaned when he stuck his thumb in my butt. "Oh yes baby."

"You like thumbs in your ass?

"Yes but I love dicks even better."

"I knew that you was a freaky bitch." Jay stuck his dick in my ass slowly inch by inch. He pumped slowly till he seen how much I could take. He sped up and started fucking the shit out of me.

"Oh yes Jay please don't stop." I arched my back throwing my ass back on his dick. Jay pulled out, "Turn around." I laid on my back throwing my legs behind my head. Jay slammed his dick inside my pussy hard. After the third pump I started squirting out everywhere.

"I'm not finished with you yet." Jay grabbed me by the hair and threw me on top of his dick. I started riding him till he busted inside of me. After that we both fell out asleep.

"Wake the fuck up now!" Jay and I was awaken by three masked men gun men with guns in our face. "Where the fuck is the money at nigga?"

Jay laughed at them and then looked at me. "Hoe you set me up!?"

Ty pulled the clip back as I got out of the bed and started dressing. "You have one second to tell me where the money at or I'm going to kill you."

The other two men started looking all over Jay's house. "Well pussy mutherfucker you might as well pull the fucking trigger then because I'm not telling you shit." Jay laughed.

I was fully dressed now. "I found it." Maine yelled from the other room. I left out of the room and looked out as I waited for them. Jabari went in the room where Ty and Jay were.

"Night Night nigga, rest in hell." Jabari said to Jay before he pulled the trigger.

Pop! Pop! Pop! Pop! I heard the gunshots, Ty, Jabari, and Maine ran out of the room running out the back door carrying a large duffle bag. I panicked and left out the front door to where my car was. Luckily there wasn't anyone outside or driving down the street. I turned on my navigation so that I didn't get lost out here and be rolling around. My hands were shaking on the steering wheel causing me to steer over into the other lane. The car blew his horn at me snapping me back into reality. Please just let Jay be dead. Please just let Jay be dead. I repeated over and over again to myself. Ty called me, "Call me when you get home." He hung up the phone before I could even say something. I drove home in silence and then I received a phone call from Tichina. Damn what does she want I thought? She knew that I was going on a date with Jay tonight. I debated on answering the phone or not. After the third ring I answered putting on my sleepy voice.

"Hello." I played like I was sleeping.

"Emani you sleep? I thought that you were going out with Jay tonight?"

"No my head started hurting so I stayed in. We're going out another time." I lied.

"Oh okay well go back to sleep and call me tomorrow." Tichina said.

"Okay bye."

I made sure that I ended the phone call and started laughing. Now everything won't fall back on me because I never got up with Jay to begin with. When I made it home Sweetie was there sitting on my couch.

"Hey Emani Ty asked me to watch the kids while you were out with your girlfriends." Sweetie said.

"Thank you Sweetie. I hope that they weren't a problem." I said playing it off.

"Oh no not at all. I guess I will go now. See you later Emani and take care."

I walked Sweetie to the front door and waved at her as she pulled off. Quickly I got out of that dress and lingerie and placed it in a bag. I ran a tub full of hot water and sat in it scrubbing Jay's scent off of me.

Chapter 18

Tyrese

We made it back to the trap house and counted the money ending up with one hundred and thirty thousand dollars. That was good shit right there but we wasn't finished yet. I've been hollering at Tootie and found out that on Monday's one of his people pick up the cash from all of Tee's businesses. In the morning we were hitting up the cleaners, hearing that was Tee's most lucrative business. Maine was cooling out sitting on the couch while Jabari was smoking a blunt. We heard someone at the door it was Sweetie and Tweety. They both were coming inside, Tweety looked high as hell, like she was off something. Sweetie was bubbly and giggling like she was high.

"I hope that you're not snorting that bullshit up yall noses." I yelled as they walked past us laughing amongst themselves. "Silly bitches."

I called Emani to make sure that she was cool. She said that she was but I could hear it in her voice that she wasn't. I'd deal with her later right now I had to get some rest so that we could hit those niggas bright and early.

Tweety and Sweetie rode together, we were using Sweetie to distract them. We were sitting in front of the cleaners. Sweetie played like she was putting some items in the cleaners to get cleaned. The young lady at the register helped her out. A guy came from the back carrying a black duffle and said goodbye to the female worker. On cue Sweetie walked away leaving out in front of him. Immediately Sweetie big ass caught his attention. The guy flirted with Sweetie, Maine and I jumped out of the car masked with our glocks pointed at his head.

"Can I help you two bitch ass niggas?" He had a mugged look on his face. I snatch the duffle bag from him. "Do you know who you're playing with? You niggas must want to die."

Pop! "I shot him in the leg. "Send him them message." We ran and jumped in the car pulling off. Everyone outside scattered and ran as well. Sweetie bailed in the car, Tweety busted a u turn. We ditched the stolen car in a remote area and bailed in our car with Tweety and Sweetie. We made it back to the trap house with the cash and started adding up the cash. Jabari stayed behind and was upset that I didn't have him apart of the mission. Last night when everyone went to sleep he stayed up and got high off the leaf. There was no way that I was going to have his high ass out there with me. Whenever he smoked that shit he would be tripping. I couldn't take a risk of him shooting me or fucking up the whole mission.

Meanwhile

My cellphone start blowing up, it was Ameeka the girl who ran my cleaners. "Tee, Lil John just got shot and robbed in front of the cleaners."

"What is he cool? Where is he now?" I jumped up and threw on shoes, grabbed my keys and my two Rugers.

"He jumped in the car and drove off. Please give him a call. Police are everywhere." Ameeka said she was cool and calm.

"Alright you know what to do, you didn't see nothing. I'll be up there to check on you. In the meantime close the place down."

"Okay Tee."

Before I could call Lil John he was calling me. He told me what happened as he drove himself to the hospital. I was furious when I heard that my little homie had got shot. The money could be replaced, but whoever pulled it with me was going to die. I told Lil John to keep me updated on his condition. After that I hit up Keith, Jay and Dee. Keith and Dee met up with me at the cleaners. Police were everywhere so we couldn't get through.

"Excuse me we're the business owners of the cleaners. We need to get through to make sure that my workers are fine." I said to a detective that I didn't recognize.

"What's your name?" The detective asked me.

"My name is not your concern. I understand that it was a shooting in front of my business." Before I could finish Detective Carr walked up. "Hello Tavion, Keith, and Dustin. It seems to be one of you missing. Where is Justin? Was your cleaners involved in this shooting? We heard the victim walked out of your cleaners, the suspects shoot him, and then drove off. Funny thing is when we showed up the victim is no longer here."

"Well that sounds like your problem and not ours Carr." Keith said.

"Let them through." Detective Carr said.

We walked past Chicago PD, Lil John blood was still on the concrete. Ameeka unlocked the doors so we can enter. "You good Ameeka?" Dee asked her.

"Yes I'm good, how is Lil John?" She was concerned about Lil John he was like a brother to her. I treated everyone that worked for me like family. I gave my staff the next two days off with pay. I had to see what was going on. We took the tapes from the recorder out back and left.

"Aye did anyone of you hear from Jay?" I asked Dee and Keith it seemed kind of strange for him not to hit us back.

"No but I'm going by his place now to check on him." Dustin jumped in his Maybach and pulled off. Keith and I went back to the slot to play the surveillance tape. It was rocking my brain on who would do this. I know that niggas was fucked up out here but how would they know our money pick up day was Monday morning. On the tape when the female walk in with some items, she seemed nervous to me. You see when Lil John walks up front, the female eyes dart over at him. It was like she was trying to get his attention because she was swinging her ass too hard. Words was exchanged and when the two masked men approached him on the outside, she calmly walks off. She never showed an expression of fear or shock. Whoever she was we were going to find her. It didn't make any sense to look up the cleaner's ticket because nine times out of ten she didn't use her real name. We blew up her face and printed out some pictures. The two masked men were dressed in all black. We couldn't pick up on any tattoos but we did see the red Chevy Impala that they were driving. I received a phone call from Dustin, what I heard on the other line made me angry. Keith and I got out of there and went over to Justin place. Someone was fucking with us and asking for a death wish.

"Whoever did is going to die!" Dee was angry and ready for revenge. Justin had been shot in the head four times. I cried as the coroner carried his lifeless body out in the body bag. His woman Shay arrived and took it hard.

"Noooooo! Please Nooooo!" She ran over to Jay body and tried to unzip the body bag. Dee pulled her back and held her.

"Why?! Please tell me this isn't real." Shay cried in his arms.

"Yes Sis it's real." They both cried.

My phone was blowing up like crazy. Apparently the news has gotten out about what happened. I called an emergency meeting with my clique. This shit was personal and we had to move fast before they strike again. Back at the slot everyone was furious about everything that went down. I passed the picture around of the female in hopes that we could find her. I handed out bullet proof vest and made sure that everyone had a least three pieces on them. If it was war that they wanted, it was a war that they were going to get. The meeting was over I had my soldiers out on the streets. Word travel fast about the killing of Twin. Englewood was dry outside on the streets, people feared for their safety and didn't want to be out when shit went down. I was angry and hurt that they took one of my brothers away. I called Dee phone several times but didn't get an answer, so instead I called Dasia's phone. When she answered the only thing that you could hear was cries over the phone.

"Is Dee cool Sis?" I asked her.

"No he's not" she muffled. We're trying our best to keep him calm Tee. Everyone is here at his mother house now." Dasia cried.

"Alright Sis, we're out here on the streets now looking for them. Do me a favor and tell him that we're on it. I'll be by there first thing in the morning."

"Tee you and Keith be safe out there. See you in the morning." Dasia said before ending the call.

All day and night we rode down on everyone's joint. The BD's didn't know who hit us. The Stones wasn't a part of it. They all sent their condolences for the loss of Jay. Even though weren't rocking with them, it was a respect thing. Everyone knew that we were about making money and if you didn't fuck with us we didn't fuck with you.

I didn't get any sleep at all last night. I looked in the mirror, my eyes were blood shoot red. I brushed my teeth and sat down trying to think about who knew the cash pick up days. My cell phones was blowing up but I refused to answer for non-irrelevant people. I wasn't ready to talk to my grandmother, I know that she would talk me out of anything that I was going to do. Tichina face time called me, I answered her call.

"Tee Oh my God are you okay, I heard what happened. Keith told Kamara and then she told me. Are you fine baby? I'm sorry about what happened to Jay. I'm really going to miss him." Tichina said.

"No baby I'm not okay but I promise you that I will be good. I promise you that won't nothing bad happen to me. I'm on my way out the door now. I will hit your line a little later on. Have a good day at work, love you."

"I love you too Tee. I'm praying for you be careful."

I made my over to the Twins mother house. It was very hard for me to face their mother Sharon right now at this moment. A lot of people were over their comforting Sharon, Dee was alone sitting on the back porch away from everyone. When Sharon saw me she smiled softly. I gave her a hug and whispered in her ear, "I'm going to kill whoever did this." Sharon patted me on the back, looked me in my eyes, "I know you will Tee." I walked through the long hallway and out the back door to join Dee. He was just sitting there stiff staring ahead of him. A bottle of Patron Gold was next to him.

"What's up Dee? We're still looking for the person who did this. I think that the robbery and Jay's death is connected." I sat in front of him as he stared off into nothing.

"Tee they shot my brother four times in the head. Whoever did it is going to wish that they could take it back. I promise I'm going to kill their mother, sister, brother and their child. I want revenge I the worse way. They will feel the same pain that I'm feeling."

"I'm with you on all of that. They're fucking with the wrong people. I won't rest till we get them."

Back At The Trap House

We counted thirty thousand dollars and added that with the one hundred thousand that we took from Jay. Damn Tee's cleaners was bring in money on a weekly basics like that. Now I see how the Jefferson's was able to move on up. We still wasn't done yet, I was anxious to hit and kill that nigga Tee. I know that getting to him was going to be hard. With the help of Emani was the only way that I was going to get close to him. The plan was to catch up with Tee when he was over Tichina's house laid up. Right now we were going to lay low and let shit die down. After everyone got their cut they were happy. Sweetie and Tweety still had work to do out there setting up other niggas. I left out to visit my new friend, it's been a few days since we've seen one another.

Buzz! Buzz! Buzz! "Who is it?" Tootie asked.

"It's Ty, let me in."

The gates to her parking lot opened up and allowed me to enter. I rolled around the parking lot until I was able to find a park. Tootie had her door opened up for me already. I gripped my nine as I entered her front door. I walked inside the house, walking straight pass her checking every room.

"Well damn! Hello to you too." Tootie snapped rolling her eyes and neck.

"I'm just making sure that we're alone. I don't trust nobody."

"What made you pop up over here, disturbing my beauty rest and shit?" Tootie was wearing a red bra and some red boy shorts.

She walked back inside her bedroom to lie down. I sat on the foot of her bed pulling out the envelope full of money. "Here's your cut of the money."

Tootie's sleepy eyes bucked out of their sockets when she held the thick envelope of money. She opened up running her fingers through the bills. "Where did this money come from?" Tootie asked sitting up in the bed.

"We hit up Jay at his place and Tee's cleaners. I used the information that you gave me."

"What?! Are you serious? When did all of this happen? I didn't hear anything about this. I always put my phone on Do Not Disturb when I'm trying to get some rest. If I don't I will not get any rest at all. How did you get close to Jay, usually the Twin's don't allow anyone to get close enough to them."

"I used Emani for to bait him in. At first I didn't think that it was going to that easy, but pussy is and always be a man weakness. We moved in on Jay and kilt him."

"Damn! I've never cared for the Twins anyway. When you get them out of the way it would be much easier to get at Tee." Tootie jumped up and gave me hug and kiss. "You the man Ty. At first I didn't think that you had the heart to do pull it."

I pushed Tootie off of me. "What you take me as a soft nigga? I've been the mother fucking man."

"I'm sorry I didn't mean no disrespect." Tootie said.

"Check it out I gotta get out of here. Keep your mouth close, it's a lot more money where that came from." I smacked Tootie on her phat ass and bounced out of there.

I went home to my baby Emani and my children. It was time for a major move in our life. A move that had to be made quickly now that all of this shit has gone down. I had to protect my family and make sure that they are safe. I've been making some secret moves by myself. You can't let your left hand know what your right hand was always doing.

Chapter 19

Tichina

Finding out that Jay was killed made me more concerned about Tee. I was afraid that I could lose him due the streets. Tee was prepared for war and made it very clearly that he wasn't going to sit back and allow anyone to just kill his friend. Word about Jay's murder traveled all the way out west. I still can't believe that Jay was killed, just the other day we were all chilling and laughing together. I was at work but my mind was on Tee and his wellbeing. If something happened to Tee I would just die. My cell phone rang and it was State Farm calling me. I wanted to curse they ass out because it's been three weeks since they have been investigating my claim. If it wasn't for Tee I wouldn't have a car to drive at all. I answered the call with an attitude prepared to speak my mind.

"Hello may I speak to Tichina Jefferson." The woman asked.

"Hi this is Tichina, how could I help you?"

"This is Nancy from State Farm Insurance Company, I'm calling in regards to your insurance claim on your 2000 Volkswagen Jetta. We're denying your claim our investigation proved that the fire was started in the tail pipe of your car. We believe that it was arson and considered it fraud."

"What?! Are you saying that I set my own car on fire? You have to be fucking kidding me. My car exploded while I was driving it." I stepped away from my desk and walked into the break room for some privacy.

"I'm sorry Miss Jefferson but we're closing your case. You have the right to file an appeal, but our investigation is accurate. If you didn't tamper with your tail pipe maybe someone else did. I suggest that you go to the police. Have a nice day." Click.

No that bitch didn't just hang up the phone on me while I was in the middle of talking. Fuck State Farm after all those years of paying my damn insurance this how they repay me. I understand that some people be doing insurance jobs, but I wasn't one of those people. Thank God I was no longer with them and decided to go with Farmers Insurance. I spent the rest of my day at work thinking about my car explosion. As soon as five pm hit I ran out of the door as fast as I could. I called Kamara to tell her what happened.

"Wow are they implying that someone put something in your tail pipe to cause your car to explode? That's some scary shit Tichina."

"Yes she insisted that I go to the police. I'm trying to figure out who would do such a thing. I don't have no enemies, well not that I know of."

"Maybe it was Emani, you never know with her. I don't put shit pass her hating ass. I have something to tell you, something that I've been holding back since I've been in the hospital."

"What is it Kamara?"

"While I was unstable I could still hear everyone but I couldn't respond. I believe that I heard Emani talking to someone about you. I don't recall what was exactly said, all I could remember hearing is Tichina and Tee."

"Are you serious Kamara? I wonder who she could've been talking to."

"It doesn't take a rocket science to figure out who she was talking to. It could've been Ty. Emani has been throwing shade ever since we got up with Tee and Keith. You're just too blinded by love to see it. Have you talked to her since Jay's death?"

"I talked to her last night, she didn't go on the date with Jay because she had a migraine. As a matter of fact I'm going to go over her house now."

I got off at the Ashland exit making my way over Emani's house. When I pulled up I seen her Jeep Cherokee parked out front. I told Kamara that I would call her back after I leave her house. Ty car wasn't outside and that was a good thing because I needed to holler at Emani one on one. I marched up the stairs and walked right inside her house. Emani's door is never locked. Her children ran to me and gave me a big hug. "Where is your mother at?" I asked them. "She's upstairs." I walked up stairs, Emani was flat ironing her hair."

"Hey what's up Tichina? I'm so glad that you're here so you can help me flat iron my hair."

"Not going to be able to do that. Emani do you know that Jay is dead?" Emani put on a fake shocked expression. That shady bitch wasn't fooling me."

233

"What?! Get the hell out of here. No I didn't I haven't heard from him since last night. How was he killed?" Emani turned around continuing to flat iron her hair like it was nothing.

"They found him inside his home shot four times in his head. Are you sure that you didn't have anything to do with his killing?" I jumped in her face so that I could have her attention.

"Are you seriously asking me if I had something to do with his killing? You have some nerves to accuse me of murder in my own home. I see you allowed Kamara put all types of bullshit in your head."

"Emani you're a hating ass bitch! You just hate the fact that Tee is spoiling and upgrading me. I bet you set my car on fire too. You're a grimey, coldhearted bitch. I don't believe shit that you say because you're such and compulsive liar."

"Tichina I don't give a fuck about what Tee does for you because without him you're just a basic, simple bitch! I didn't set your raggedy ass Volkswagen on fire, whoever did set your car on fire did you a favor. Get your dumb ass out of my face and out of my house before I beat the fuck out of you!"

Emani stood up and challenged me to hit her. "Bitch consider our friendship over with!"

I stormed out of there. Emani was close on my heels and shoved me down her stairs. I turned around and threw the bitch over the banister. Emani fell, lying on her back with her children crying over her body. She was still moving and was going to be okay because it was only a 2 foot fall and her floor was carpeted. I left out her house slamming her door causing the stained glass to shatter. I hopped in my car and sped off in a rage. If I find out that Emani had anything to do with my car exploded or the death of Jay, I swear before God I will kill that Shiesty bitch. I called Kamara to tell her went all went down. She was ready to beat Emani's ass, but you know what I had a plan for that ass baby. Emani fucked up big time when she crossed me. I'm going to destroy her life, she's going to wish that she never turned on me with her stupid ass.

The Funeral

Today was Justin aka Jay's funeral, it was being held at
Leaks & Sons Funeral Home off 78th and Cottage Grove.
Kamara and I pulled up and parked my Range with the
other foreign whips. It was so many women there dressed
like they were going to the club instead of a funeral. They
were rocking mini dresses, high heels, and so much
makeup that they look as though they should be in the
coffin. We laughed at the bullshit and went inside. As I
stepped in I seen Tee and Keith and we worked our way to
the front to have a seat. Shay was sitting next to the Twin's
mother crying on her shoulder. Suddenly I felt bad for
allowing Emani and Jay to hook up. Tee, Keith, Dee and
the rest of the men were wearing black shades and Armani
suits. I held Tee hand as the pastor began to preach. Twenty
minutes into the funeral a scantily dressed women ran
toward Jay's casket falling out and shit. To make the
situation even crazier she turned around to hit Shay but
instead she hit the Twin's mother. Security picked her up
with her dress over her head displaying all her pussy and

ass. I can't believe the ratchetness that was going on at this funeral. I was so happy that it was finally over with. Tee and Keith was pallbearers and Dee was an honorary pallbearer. The burial was held at Oakridge, it was a large crowd that attended. It didn't take long for them to place him in the ground. We all headed back to a hall for the Repass. I sat at the table with Dasia, it was my first time seeing her since the barbecue.

"How are you doing Dasia?" I sincerely asked her.

"I'm just trying to maintain and keep my family together. I have to keep an eye on Dee because I don't want to lose him too."

"I know that's right. Just ask God to give you the strength to make it through all of this. I'll keep you in my prayers."

Kamara went to make some plates of food, but I sat there talking to Dasia. I watched Tee out the corner of my eye talking to that bitch Tootie. He looked like he was irritated and didn't have a word to say to her. I excused myself from the table telling Dasia that I would be right back. I walked over to Tee and Tootie who now was giving him a hug.

"Excuse me aren't we mighty thirsty, the drinks are over there." I pulled Tootie off of Tee and pointed to the right of the room.

"Bitch you better keep your hands to yourself before you get fucked up!" Tootie said.

I laughed in her face. "Take your old ass on somewhere. Tee doesn't want you so please find you some business before you get fucked up."

"Tee get your woman!" Tootie said.

"Tootie get the hell on with that bullshit that you trying to pull. As a matter of fact leave, you're no longer welcomed here."

Several men jumped up to escort her out of the hall. Tootie was pissed off as the one of the men tried to touch her. "Don't put your mother fucking hands on me! Fuck you Tee and you know what fuck Jay too!" Tootie screamed.

No she didn't say fuck Jay too, why did she say that. Dee rushed a crossed the room and smacked the shit out of Tootie. Tootie fell to the floor and was dragged out of there and thrown on the concrete sidewalk in front of the hall. Everyone looked in shocked as we watched Dee turn into the Incredible Hulk. Dasia walked in the back to calm him down.

"Tee we need to talk right now." I said with a serious face.

We went into a room where it was a sofa and a desk.

"Tee I don't know how I can tell you this but I think. "Tee we need you right now, Dee is outside waving his gun threatening to kill Tootie." A man busted inside the room.

Tee ran out of the room to see what was going on. I went over to join Kamara.

"What the hell is going on? I was in the middle of talking to Tee and then this shit happens. As I was talking we heard gunshots outside. Everyone panicked and dropped to the floor. Me and Kamara ran toward the back leaving out the back door. We were in the alley but a lot closer to my truck. Once I got inside I pulled off, you can hear police sirens from everywhere. I rode up the block to see if I could find Tee. Kamara spotted him and Keith before me and pointed them out. They were all getting into their cars and leaving with Dee. From a distance I could see someone lying on the ground. When I got closer I seen Tootie lying on the ground next to her car bleeding from her chest. She was still alive and talking to another woman.

239

"Wow, I can't believe that Dee actually shot her." Kamara said as we rolled by.

"That's what that bitch get. She was foul for saying fuck Jay. She was mad disrespectful for that bullshit. She should've known better than that."

My day was over with for being on the Southside. I rode home and due to the time I was stuck in all the traffic. It took us two hours to get home. It was late, like around eleven pm when I received a text message from Tee letting me know that he was straight. I felt good hearing from him and knowing that he was still alive.

Me: I love u bighead ☐

Tee: I love u too

Me: Be safe out there, goodnight ☐

After that I fell asleep.

Chapter 20

Emani

After I snapped out of the fall that I took over the banister Tichina was long gone. I swear I'm going to get that bitch back real soon. My hair was fucked up and I had a knot in the back of my head from the fall. I told Ty what happened and he thought that Tichina was just fucking with me and didn't actually no shit.

"I'm trying to tell you that she knows Ty. I've been best friends with Tichina and Kamara for over twenty years. I know them bitches like the back of my hands."

"They don't know shit. She's accusing you of blowing up her car, which is a fucking lie. What she's trying to do is fish for some bullshit and you let her." Ty said.

Ty could be right about that. Honestly I didn't have anything to do with Tichina's car. I already know that Kamara was behind putting that bullshit in her head. There was no way that they could implicate me to Jay's murder. After everything that went down Ty came home with all types of surprises. One was my cash that I earned from setting up Jay. The second was us moving to a house in Aurora. Apparently Ty has hid this house from me that he's been renting out for the past six months. It's funny how you think you know the person that you've been sleeping with for five years. First the secret insurance policy and now the secret house. We were packing the things that we were taking with us. Ty said that the place was already furnished. I'm giving the old furniture away to whoever wants it in my family. Ty made me promise not to tell anyone where we was going. I spend the hours packing and calling around for a moving company. Everyone was booked up except one moving company, but they couldn't move us until the end of the week on Friday. Ty was cool with that and so was I because all of this was happening fast. Throughout the week I kept a low profile, only going to work and coming home. I took my money over Big Momma house and placed it under her mattress where I know it was safe at. No one ever went into Big Momma's room ever without her being present. I haven't heard from Tichina or Kamara, they both deleted me as their friend off social media and their lives. Word around town was that Tee and his crew had a twenty thousand dollar reward out for Jay's murder.

With that type of money I'm more than sure that everyone was trying to find the killer.

Jabari

Jabari was on cloud nine after getting his cash up since the resent murder of Jay and the other hits that they did. He was feeling himself and blowing through his money like it grew on trees. At the present moment he was at the Fifty Yard Line buying out the bar. Jabari was drunk and talking major shit like he always did.

"Fuck that nigga Jay! His bitch ass thought that he was untouchable." Jabari laughed almost falling off the bar stool. "I put that nigga in hell." Jabari acted like he was shooting four gunshots to the head.

Everyone watched as he carried on the show. A young men in the back pulled out his phone to make a call. "Yo this is Kenny, I need to holler at Tee about the Jay's death." One of the soldiers handed Tee their phone.

"What's up Kenny?" Tee said ready to hear some good news.

"Yo Tee I'm up here at the Fifty Yard Line and it's some clown ass nigga up here bragging about killing Jay. He talking big shit man, going into to details and everything and flashing money around."

"Were on our way up there now. Keep an eye on him till we get there." Tee hung up the phone.

Everyone grabbed their bangers and jumped in their whips. Hopefully he was the killer or could point us to the killers because lately the calls haven't been accurate that they have been receiving. Everyone was calling and just dropping names just for the cash reward. Tee and his crew wasn't any fools and didn't go off just any bullshit that they heard. From where they slot was located it didn't take any time getting up to the Fifty Yard Line. Tee called Kenny, he picked up right away.

"Is he still up there?" Tee asked.

"Yes he's still at the bar drinking." Kenny said.

"Put the bartender on the phone real quick." Tee hollered at the bartender and told her to have security to put Jabari out. She gave Kenny back his phone and did what she was told.

Jabari was told that he had reached his minimum and was asked to leave. He didn't put up a fight, "Fuck ya'll I'll spend my money elsewhere." Jabari staggered out the door pulling out a Newport and lighting it up. He walked to his car and jumped in behind the wheel drunk, puffing on his cigarette. Before he put his key in the ignition Jabari felt the cold piece of steel pointed in the back of his head.

"Silly nigga you're going with us." The man said.

"I'm not going no damn where. Do what the fuck you got to now." Jabari said he tried to reach for his piece but was knocked out by the gun and dragged out of his car.

An hour later Jabari woke up with a spitting headache and a bag over his head. His arms and legs were tied to a wooden chair. He was only dressed in his boxers and was wearing Jay's custom made gold chain with the letter J embedded in diamonds around his neck. During the robbery Jabari stole his chain and rocked it like it was his since both of their initials started with J. The bag was removed from his head. Tee and Keith stood in front of him dressed in all black from head to toe. Jabari laughed, he was now aware of who kidnapped him and why.

"Kill me now because I'm not going to talk. I'm not no rat." Jabari said.

"Why did you do it?" Keith asked.

"What type of dumb question is that?! Shit for the mother fucking money that's why." Jabari laughed and spat on the floor.

"I know that you had some help. Who helped you? Tee asked.

"Look I'm not telling you shit so kill me now." Jabari said.

Tee grew angry, he had no other choice but to kill him. Although he wanted to kill this hoe ass nigga himself, he didn't want to take the pleasure away from Dee. They called Dee to tell him that they had one of Jay's killer. Dee rushed over there quickly and was amped up. When he seen Jabari wearing his brother gold chain he went insane. He removed his brother's chain from around Jabari's neck and let several rounds off into his body.

Tyrese

I've been trying to hit up Jabari for the last two days but haven't heard from him. Every time when we came up with some money he always fell back from us for a few days. Shit was beginning to piss me off because I couldn't get in touch with Tootie either. I called Bari girlfriend number looking for him, but she didn't answer. It was still early in the morning, maybe she was still sleep. We were all chilling at the trap house on rainy morning. Sweetie and Tweety were still working on the next tricks that we planned to hit up soon. Maine and I was busy in the kitchen putting in work. With the cocaine that I had copped from Duke we put that out on the streets and managed to flip that shit. I finally had money pouring in, enough to take care of my family. I was thinking about opening up a business as well, maybe I will open up a cleaners like Tee on the Westside. Hell he had so much money flowing in, I think that I would consider that. Maine placed the money in the bill machine, as the machine counted the money I received a phone call. I looked at the number on the phone, it was Bari girlfriend calling me back.

"Ty he's dead." She cried on the phone,

"Who's dead?" I asked her.

"Jabari they killed him, I woke up this morning with his head in my bed. What is going on Ty? What did you do?!" She cried and screamed into the phone.

"You found only his head and not his torso?" I asked her.

"Only his fucking head! These people came into my house where my children and I are sleeping. They could've killed us. Oh my God, I have to call the police." She cried.

Stacy got up to check on her children to make sure that they were still in their rooms. Her daughter and son was still sleeping in their beds unharmed. She walk through the house to check out if anyone else was still there. Her house was empty and her doors were locked as if anyone hasn't entered her home. She looked out the window and discovered Bari's torso sitting on their front porch. Stacy screamed dropping her cell phone on the floor leaving Ty on the phone. Ty heard her cries and hollered her name. "Stacy! Stacy! Stacy what is it?!"

Kamara

With everything that has been going on in the streets Keith spent minimum time with me. I was understanding and stood by my man side. I was surprise that he showed up at my place last night. Keith arrived after one pm damn near scaring the shit out of me. I pulled my pistol out on him but lowered it once I realized that it was him. Happy to see him and more than thankful that he was still alive, I jumped all over him. Last night I catered to my man in every type of way. I know that everything was stressing him out so I had to make him feel good. Keith wasn't supposed to be laid up with me because of everything that was going on. He was a grown ass man and at a time like this only I could bring the calmness that he needed in his life right now. It was going on six am when Keith rolled over. His phone was blowing up like crazy. I looked at the caller on his phone and seen that it was Tee calling him. I shook him to wake him up, maybe it was important. Keith answered his phone half asleep. After the call he got up to brush his teeth and to wash his face. He didn't have time to shower and eat.

While Keith was putting on his jeans a piece of folded paper fell out of his back pocket. I picked it up and unfolded it trying to be nosy. As I unfolded the paper it was a picture of the girl who be running up behind Ty all the time.

"What are you doing with this in your back pocket?" I held the piece of paper up in front of Keith.

"Be cool baby, it's not what you think. It's a picture of the girl who we think was a part of the robbery at Tee's cleaners last week."

"Really I know her. Well I don't know her exactly, but I do know that she's from out west." I said.

"Are you serious?! Do you know her name?! Fuck that, I don't need her name. Do you know where she hangs out at?" Keith anxiously wanted to know.

"Hold up let me call Tichina, she can help you better than I can."

I called Tichina waking her up out of her sleep. I explained to her what was going on and I handed the phone to Keith so that they could talk. Keith hollered at Tichina and listened to everything that she told him. After he ended the call with her, he called Tee. Tee was pleased with the news and made his way out west.

Two hours later Tee was over my place. He spoke with Tichina, but she wasn't able to call off work today. Tichina called Tee back and told him that she was able to leave at noon. From the information that Tichina provided she told us that the girl Sweetie works for Ty. Tee and Keith didn't know who Ty was and where he came from. I had to break everything down to them since Tichina wasn't here.

"Sweetie is one of the girls who works for Ty. Ty is in the business of setting up niggas with money. Ty is Emani's man."

Keith cut me off. "Your friend Emani?" he asked.

"Ex friend, Tichina and I cut her ass off last week. Anyway Ty is Emani's man. Emani may have been going back telling information to Ty."

"Wait but how? I never told Tichina where my cleaners was. Whoever knew that was someone that I've known for a long time."

"Maybe Emani didn't have anything to do with the robbery, but I do feel that she had something to do with the death of Jay." I said.

"Why do you think that?" Keith asked.

"Because the night that Jay was killed him and Emani had a date. Tichina called Emani that night to see how the date was going, but Emani said that she cancelled because she had a migraine."

"Wait a minute, I hollered at Jay that night and he was on a date with Emani. He said that he was with Tichina's girl." Tee said, he jumped up.

"Where does Emani live?" Tee asked.

I gave them Emani's address. Tee and Keith ran out of my house and jumped in his car. I was confused, I didn't know what was going on. I called Tichina several times but she didn't answer her phone.

Chapter 21

Emani

I called off work today so that I could get as much packing done as I could. It was Wednesday the movers will be here on Saturday. Tyshawn stayed at home with me, Lil Ty and Tyeisha was over Big Momma's house. Tyshawn and I packed as much as could in two hours. After that I cooked us something to eat to fill up our bellies. I had spoken to Ty on the phone and he didn't sound right.

"Ty what's up? Why do you sound strange is it something going on that I should know about?" I asked Ty.

"No, I'm trying to catch up with Bari. I haven't seen him in two days, that's all."

"Well maybe you should call his girl Stacy. You know how Bari acts when he gets some money." I said.

"I'll do that, how's the packing coming along?" Ty asked.

"Cool, it would be better if you were here to help out." I said with an attitude.

"Baby you know that I have to make the money. I promise after we move I will spend more time with you and the children."

"Okay well you be cool out there and keep your head up at all times. I love you."

"I love you too Emani. I wouldn't be able to pull all of this without you." Ty said.

I ended the call and continued to pack. Two hours later I was burned out and needed to stop. I was pretty much finished with everything. I only had the kitchen left to pack. Tyshawn asked if he could go outside to play next door with the neighbor's children. I allowed him to and went upstairs to run me some bath water so I could soak. When the water was done I got inside the tub, sat back and relaxed. I turned off everything in the house and wanted peace and quietness. After all the chaos that was going on I needed a fucking break from it all. As I soaked in the tub I could hear someone downstairs inside my home. I figured it was Ty, but after a while I could hear whoever it was whispering. I panicked and got out of the tub, grabbing a towel and wrapping it around me. I also grabbed my phone and tiptoed out of the bathroom. By that time I was walking down my hallway to see what was going on. I peeped down the stairway and seen Tee and Keith dressed in all black with their guns drawn. Keith and I made eye contact and I took off down the hallway and back stairs. They were on my heels as I ran out my back door into my back yard. It was raining out and not a person in sight. I hopped my gate as bullets flew past me barely missing me by inches. I zigzagged down the alley so that the bullets didn't hit me. I ran off into a vacant building and hid inside there. I could hear Tee and Keith as they searched the vacant building. I turned my phone off so that it didn't ring and make any noises. I shivered and cried with my hands over my mouth as they both got closer to me. I prayed silently in my head.

"Lord please don't let them catch me. Lord please protect me right now."

I was hiding underneath a pile of wood staring at their shoes. Lucky for me they walked away and left out of the building. I stayed hidden and naked wrapped in my bath towel under the pile of wood making sure that they were gone. When the coast was clear I pulled out my phone to call Ty. He picked up quickly.

"Ty they came to the house looking for us. I got away and ran out the backdoor." I cried.

"Who did?! Where are you and Tyshawn at right now?" Ty angrily asked.

"I'm hiding in the vacant house on the next block. Tyshawn is over at the neighbor house, I sent him there to play. Ty please come get me. I'm naked with a bath towel wrapped around me." I cried.

"I'll be there in a minute. Stay right there until I get there baby." Ty said.

I was crying and shivering cold. It was the end of summer out and the rain didn't make it any better. I wiped away my tears and waited patiently for Ty to come and get me.

Tichina

I was on my way off work early because Kamara, Tee, and Keith were waiting on me at her place. The first person that I called was Tee but he didn't answer, so after that I called Kamara. Kamara answered the phone and told me everything that went down in my absence. I was shocked that they were on their way to Emani's place. We all know what was going to happen once they arrived there. It was during the work week, I knew for sure that Emani was at work and that the children were away. Damn now everything was starting to make sense to me. Kamara was right about Emani shady ass all this time. I was too blind to see that she was playing me all along. I would have never thought that Emani would betray me after all these years. As far as I'm concerned she is already considered dead to me, so if they kill her it wouldn't even matter. After hearing about what Tee was on I didn't bother to call him again. He already knew that I was getting off work at noon, I would just wait for him over at Kamara's house. When I approached the Ashland exit traffic started to pile up. It was an accident so I decided to get off, take the streets so far, and then jump back on the expressway. I didn't have time to be sitting in no damn traffic. When I got off, I was cruising down Congress when I was cut off by a black Tahoe truck.

"With the fuck!" I looked at who was driving the truck, but they had on mask.

I was blocked in and couldn't go forward or reverse. Instead I got out of my truck and jetted for it. I kicked off my heels and ran for my life as the two masked men chased me down the street. I was screaming help but no one heard my screams. Due to the rain there wasn't many people outside. The masked men were catching up with me.

Pow! **Pow**! **Pow**! The starting shooting at me. One of the bullets caught me in the leg causing me to fall to the ground. The masked gun men stood over me.

Pow! They shot me once in the chest. They were prepared to shoot me again but someone screamed they're shooting outside.

The masked men ran off leaving me on the ground. "Help! Help!" I screamed as I laid on the ground. The rain was coming down hard on me. I prayed that someone will hear my cries. I tried to move and blanked out. A woman ran outside her house and covered my body as she called 911. The paramedics arrived and quickly rushed me to Stroger Hospital. I had been shot inches away from my heart.

Tyrese

Hopefully that bitch Tichina is dead. I wanted to put a few more rounds in her but someone heard us. I can't go down for murder so Maine and I got out of there. Emani was still waiting on us in the vacant house so I had to scoop her up. It just so happened that we ran into Tichina on our way over there and decided to drive down on her. I pulled up cautiously making sure that Tee and Keith weren't still around. I went into the vacant house to go get Emani while Maine looked out. Emani was balled up under the wood wrapped in a bath towel. When she seen me she jumped into my arms crying.

"It's okay. I'm here now, you don't have anything to worry about."

"What the fuck took you so long?!" Emani angrily said, she was shivering cold.

"I'm here now." I carried her out of the house and put her into the truck.

Emani cell phone rang, she answered it.

"Hello." Emani said.

A deep male voice said on the phone. "We have your deaf son. If you want to see him alive you have to trade your life for his. You have twenty four hours to meet me at 5555 East Sangamon."

"Noooo!" Emani screamed. "They have Tyshawn!"

CPSIA information can be obtained
at www.ICGtesting.com
Printed in the USA
LVOW04s1748021216
515533LV00010B/911/P